Karen had walked down the aisle and sat down before her words really hit Lorie. They came in funny little waves, almost like ocean waves that got bigger and bigger as Lorie understood them better. As the words finally washed over her, she almost shouted, "Wait! Not me!"

☆☆☆☆☆☆☆☆☆☆☆☆☆☆☆☆☆☆☆☆☆☆☆☆☆☆☆☆☆

LORIE FOR PRESIDENT

☆☆☆☆☆☆☆☆☆☆☆☆☆☆☆☆☆☆☆☆☆☆☆☆☆☆☆☆☆

by Elizabeth Van Steenwyk

Cover photo by John Strange

Published by Willowisp Press, Inc.
401 E. Wilson Bridge Road, Worthington, Ohio 43085

Copyright ©1988 by Willowisp Press, Inc.

All rights reserved. No portion of this book may be reproduced, stored in a retrieval system, or transmitted, in any form or by any means, electronic, mechanical, photocopying, recording, or otherwise without prior written permission from the publisher.

Printed in the United States of America

10 9 8 7 6 5 4 3 2 1

ISBN 0-87406-322-1

One

LORIE Scott looked down Wembly Road, waiting to see Melissa turn the corner and hurry toward her. The two good friends had met this way every day of the school year since third grade. This morning, their first day at junior high, they had agreed to meet 10 minutes earlier. They wanted extra time to find their lockers and homerooms—and possibly even meet some new kids from the other elementary schools. Lorie paced up and down, jittery and nervous.

There she was! Melissa rounded the corner and casually strolled along in her new jeans as if they were still going to Weston Elementary and this was just another day in sixth grade. *That's Melissa Whitner for you,* Lorie thought, *cool and with it.* All this new stuff didn't bother her.

Lorie ran to meet her. "Hurry up," she

called. "We've got to find our lockers and get to homeroom and. . . ."

Melissa smiled as Lorie coasted to a stop in front of her. "Look," Melissa said. "I got my ears pierced." She pulled her straight, blond hair back so Lorie could see.

Lorie looked closely at the little gold stars in Melissa's ears. "Did it hurt?" she asked.

"Of course not." Melissa swung her new book bag over her shoulder as they fell in step together. "You ought to do it, Lorie. It makes you look much older."

"Well, maybe I will later this year." Lorie walked a little faster, hoping Melissa would pick up her pace, too. "Right now I've got enough to worry about."

"It's only junior high school," Melissa said. "You're a good student. You shouldn't have any problems."

"It's not grades I'm worried about. It's all those new kids . . . I won't know any of them."

"You'll get acquainted." Melissa made it sound easy. "Just think about all the cute guys you're going to meet."

Lorie smiled. She liked that idea all right.

"You can join all kinds of clubs," Melissa went on. "At least that's what Bob said."

"Bob?" Lorie asked.

"Bob Quigley. You know, he lives next door

to me, and he's in eighth grade this year. His family came over for a cookout last night, and he told me about all the stuff that goes on at junior high."

"For instance?"

"Like electing class officers, which happens practically right away."

"Electing officers?" Lorie repeated. "Oh, Melissa, I'm going to nominate you for . . . I don't know. What do you want to be?"

"Gee, thanks, Lor." Melissa swung her book bag a couple of times. "I guess I'd go for president."

As they continued on their way, Lorie looked into the maple trees overhead. Lacy patches of blue sky peeked through the leaves that were already showing hints of autumn weather. Soon the leaves would turn bright gold and red. Maybe by that time, she'd feel better about the new school.

Nearing Huntington Junior High, Lorie saw more of their friends from Weston Elementary. Then suddenly there were so many faces she didn't know.

Don't panic, she told herself. But she began to feel so nervous that she wanted to jump right out of her skin.

"What are you thinking about?" asked Melissa. "Come on, tell me."

"I was just thinking about what I'd look like if I didn't have any skin on," Lorie said. Then she gave a slight giggle.

"You're crazy," Melissa said. But she laughed too, and they continued up the sidewalk to the front of the school, trying to control a general attack of the sillies. *Nothing's changed so far,* Lorie thought. *We're just as crazy as we were last year at Weston!*

Inside the main corridor, however, they quieted down in a hurry. Even Melissa seemed a little awed. Everything seemed so big— bigger, at least, than Weston. The noise of locker doors opening and slamming shut echoed through the long hall.

"We'll never find our lockers," Lorie whispered, more to herself than Melissa.

"Yes, we will. Remember that letter we got last week said that seventh graders have lockers in the hall leading to the cafeteria. Bob said we just follow our noses."

Lorie let Melissa lead as they threaded their way through the milling crowd in the main corridor. When the cafeteria sign appeared suddenly, Lorie sighed as she followed Melissa into the smaller, quieter hall. Lorie found her locker first.

"Mine must be further along this way," Melissa said, and she continued walking.

"Wait," Lorie shouted. "I'll walk with you to homeroom."

Melissa turned around. "That's okay. We're not in the same one anyway," she said. "So what's the point of waiting? I'll see you in the cafeteria at lunch."

After she was gone, Lorie felt terribly alone. She began to dial the locker combination numbers which she had memorized. The combination clicked open on the first try. A stale odor of orange peel greeted her.

Lorie didn't know what to do next. She glanced around to see what others were doing.

One girl had hooked a mirror on her locker door and was brushing her hair. Good idea. A boy, two lockers down, was stuffing in a football, shoulder pads, and helmet. No help there. Another girl was pasting pictures of rock stars on the inside of her locker door, while someone else had a poster of a movie star.

"Hey, Lorie, how's it going?"

Lorie nearly jumped out of her socks as she whirled around. "Buzz Howard," she exclaimed. "You scared me."

"It doesn't take much with you." He laughed. As usual he was wearing his L.A. Dodgers baseball cap and a California Angels sweatshirt. *Doesn't he have any other clothes?* Lorie wondered.

9

"It's about time for homeroom to start," he said. "Come on, I'll walk you."

"How do you know what homeroom I'm in?" Lorie asked.

"You've only told me about a dozen times this week," he said. " 'I'm in Mr. Crawford's homeroom,' " he repeated, doing his best imitation of her. "Come on, it's right down the hall here, next to my homeroom."

Lorie relaxed a little as she walked with Buzz. Good old Buzz—they'd been neighbors since first grade, and he was pretty easy to be around.

"Here you go," Buzz said.

"I don't know a single person," Lorie whispered.

"Someone's bound to turn up," Buzz said. "So long."

"Excuse me," someone said behind her. Lorie stepped aside so a couple of girls could enter.

"Are you going in or what?" another voice asked. Lorie turned to see a short boy staring at her.

"Yes," she mumbled. Lorie gulped hard and stepped inside, then sat down quickly in the first empty seat she found.

Lorie concentrated hard on watching Mr. Crawford write on the chalkboard. It was easier than looking around and having to talk to someone.

My name is Mr. Crawford, his printing read. *This is Homeroom 22.* The tall, thin man adjusted his red bow tie when he finished writing.

Lorie pulled her class schedule out and studied it, even though she knew it by heart. Math first period, then social studies, Spanish, and lunch period. Her lunch money! Lorie realized it was still lying on the kitchen table at home. She had been so nervous this morning that she had forgotten it!

"Oh, no," she groaned quietly, digging through her book bag for spare change. She found a quarter and dug for more. Nothing.

Someone tapped her shoulder. "I said, what's the matter?"

Lorie turned around and looked into the greenest eyes she'd ever seen. The girl who had tapped Lorie on the shoulder had shining, short, black hair cut in the latest style, and a tan that looked fresh from a recent beach vacation.

"I—I guess I forgot my lunch money," Lorie stammered.

"Here, I have some you can borrow." The girl pulled a couple of dollar bills from her purse and held them out.

Lorie hesitated, then took the money.

"Thanks a lot. I'll pay you back tomorrow," Lorie said.

"Whenever. My name's Karen Bradley. What's yours?"

"Lorie Scott. I'm from Weston School."

"I'm from New York," Karen said.

"You mean New York state or New York City?"

"Both." Karen laughed. "My dad was transferred here by his company. He's executive vice president of The Best Department Store."

"Wow," Lorie breathed. The Best was the most exclusive store in town. Her mom always said it cost her money just to walk through the door and look.

"What does your dad do?" Karen asked. She pulled at a tangle of gold chains around her neck.

"He . . ." Lorie paused. "He owns a kind of fast-food restaurant."

"Which one?" Karen asked.

"The Quick Chick," Lorie said. "It's a charbroiled chicken place."

"I've never heard of it," Karen said. "But I'm sure I'll like it. Why don't we go there on Saturday for lunch?"

"I have to help Mom clean the house on

Saturday." Lorie just said the first thing that popped into her head.

"I'll help you," Karen said. "Then we can go have lunch at your dad's place. Oh, this is great. We just moved to this town and I've already found a friend!"

Lorie turned around as Mr. Crawford cleared his throat to get everybody's attention. *How did I get to be her friend so fast?* she wondered. *Because she loaned me money? And how does she know I want to be friends with her?"*

Mr. Crawford kept clearing his throat and adjusting his bow tie as he waited for some boys in the back to settle down. Lorie thought about Karen. *It would be neat to be able to make friends with people that easily. And it would be great to look like her, too, especially to own those clothes. Everything she wears is probably the best of The Best.*

Finally Mr. Crawford began to talk, making announcements about library cards and cafeteria schedules and seating assignments for homeroom. "If you like where you're sitting, then that's your assigned seat," he said. Again he pulled on his bright red tie.

Lorie glanced around to see Karen smiling at her. "Good," the dark-haired girl whispered. "I was afraid he'd separate us."

Lorie turned back to the front after hearing

another throat-clearing "Harumpff" from Mr. Crawford. "This week we'll get acquainted. Next week we elect seventh-grade officers," he said. "Get to know the new kids in your classes, think about your old friends from last year, and be prepared to nominate someone who shows leadership and responsibility. There are three seventh-grade homerooms, and there should be one nomination from each for every office."

"Can we nominate someone we know who's in another homeroom?" a girl asked.

"Sure." Mr. Crawford nodded. "Now remember, we need six qualified nominees: a president, vice president, secretary, treasurer, and two representatives to the student council."

"I know who I'm going to nominate for president," Karen whispered.

Lorie turned around, wondering. *That means Karen must know at least one other person in school besides me,* Lorie thought.

"I know someone I'm going to nominate, too," Lorie whispered back, thinking of Melissa.

As Lorie turned again to face the front of the room, she had a horrifying thought. *What if Karen thinks I'm going to nominate her?*

Two

"ISN'T it great that all our morning classes are together?" Karen asked as she followed Lorie to the cafeteria at noon.

"Ummm," Lorie said. She secretly wished that Karen wouldn't always pick the seats where both of them sat in each class. Lorie had wanted to sit next to someone she'd known from Weston. Probably it didn't matter, though. By tomorrow most of the teachers would have seating charts and assigned seats anyway.

Now Lorie looked forward to seeing Melissa in the cafeteria. She wanted to talk to her about the class nominations right away. Lorie paused to look for Melissa just inside the entrance.

"Come on, Lorie, let's get in line," Karen said. "I want taco pizza and it might be gone if we stand around and let other kids beat us to it."

"But I was looking for a friend," Lorie began.

"You can look for her in line," Karen said, twisting her gold chains. "Come on, we'll save a place for her."

"Well, okay." Lorie started for the taco pizza line with Karen, meanwhile looking around the room. Had she missed seeing Melissa? There were so many kids now. Or what if her lunch period was different?

"Hey, Lorie, looking for someone?"

"Melissa!" Lorie almost shouted. "Am I glad to see you. I haven't seen you once this morning."

"All kids in band have their classes scheduled together because Mr. Kelly, the music teacher, only comes in the afternoons. We won't be seeing each other much in classes."

"Oh, brother," Lorie said. "Now I'll never see you."

"Hi," Karen said. "Are you a friend of Lorie's, too?"

"This is my best friend, Melissa Whitner," Lorie said. "Melissa, this is Karen Bradley. She's in my homeroom and—"

"How long have you been best friends?" Karen interrupted.

"Forever," Melissa said. "We've been best

friends so long I can't remember when we weren't. Can you, Lorie?"

"That must be neat," Karen said. "I guess we moved too much for me to have a friend that long."

"That's too bad," Lorie said. "I hope you don't have to move for a long, long time now."

"Do you mean it, Lorie? That's super." Karen grabbed Lorie's arm, then stepped in between to take Melissa's arm, too. "Now let's get some taco pizza."

Lorie felt herself being moved along by Karen, wishing she'd had a chance to talk to Melissa alone. She glanced over Karen's head at Melissa. They were both much taller than Karen. Melissa grinned and raised her eyebrows, then shrugged helplessly. Lorie shrugged back. That always seemed to be their secret signal that said *We'll talk this over later.*

"Where did you turn into such a taco pizza freak?" Lorie asked Karen as they moved through the food line.

"When we lived in California," Karen said. "Sometimes on Saturdays, Dad and I would go out and get it for lunch."

"I thought you moved here from New York," Lorie said.

"I did, but we lived in California before that."

"Did I hear someone say something about my favorite vacation spot?" Buzz suddenly appeared beside them.

Karen looked at his shirt and cap. "You can't make up your mind which California baseball team to pull for, can you?"

"If it's from California, I root for it," Buzz said, smiling down at her. "Which team do you like best?"

"I can't stand baseball," Karen said. "It's so boring."

"Maybe if you had an expert explain it to you, it wouldn't be so boring." Buzz was trying to act like Mr. Cool, Lorie decided, holding back a giggle.

"If I ever find an expert, I'll do just that," Karen said. She winked at Lorie as she turned her back on Buzz and reached for a tray.

Buzz's face turned down with disappointment. "Oh," he said, backing away.

Lorie suddenly felt sorry for him. *Why did Karen act like that toward Buzz? Is this how you treat guys in junior high?*

Melissa raised her eyebrows at Lorie, indicating that she, too, had noticed.

Karen smiled at both of the girls. "Now where shall we sit?"

* * * * *

Afternoon classes moved quickly, and Lorie's tension nearly disappeared by the time she returned to her locker at the end of the day. *Maybe junior high won't be so bad,* she thought, working her combination.

She opened her locker door and threw a few books inside, but her math and social studies books remained in her bag. Homework, already! It didn't take the teachers long.

Melissa hurried up to her. "I'm starving," she said. "Got anything to eat in there?" She poked around in Lorie's locker.

"No, but that's not a bad idea." She slammed the door shut and they began to walk down the hall. They headed for the nearest double doors and walked outside. The day was still warm, and the air felt soft and soothing. Lorie was looking forward to being alone with Melissa for a while. They had so much to talk about, and Lorie still hadn't had a chance to talk to Melissa about the elections.

"So what did I tell you about the first day?" Melissa asked as they walked down the sidewalk. "It wasn't so bad, was it?"

Lorie started to answer, but stopped before a word came out of her mouth. She saw Karen waving to her from the corner. "Look," Lorie said. "Who's that waving to us?"

"It looks like Karen," Melissa said. "Did you know she was going to wait for you?"

"No," Lorie said. "What do you suppose she wants?"

"I have no idea." Melissa shrugged.

"Hi," Karen said as they approached her. "Bet you're surprised to see me."

"Just a little." Lorie began to unbutton her sweater, feeling warm.

"Actually I live out in this direction." Karen squeezed in between them as they walked toward the corner. "Besides, it's boring to walk alone. I'm glad I can join you two all the time."

"The only time I ever walked home alone was in third grade when Lorie had the chicken pox," Melissa said.

"Aren't there any cute guys to walk with around here?" Karen asked.

"Bob, my next-door neighbor, is kind of cute," Melissa said. Her face brightened as she spoke.

"Have you got a crush on him?" Karen asked.

"Of course not!" Melissa answered. "He's just a guy next door."

"Have either of you ever had a date?" Karen asked, matching her stride to theirs.

Melissa glanced at Lorie before she shook her head.

"Have *you* ever had a date?" Melissa asked Karen.

Karen readjusted the books she was carrying before she answered. "Sure. You don't think I'm a square, do you?"

"You mean your mom let you go out alone with a boy?" Lorie couldn't believe it.

"In the daytime, I'll bet," Melissa said. "Not at night."

"Well. . . ." Karen paused before she finally answered. "Once, it was almost dark when we got out of the movies. It was a double feature."

Melissa rolled her eyes meaningfully at Lorie while Lorie wondered if she could believe Karen. She had a lot to talk over with Melissa.

Karen continued to do most of the talking as they walked along now. But the walking wasn't easy as they tried to walk three across. *Sidewalks are made for two people, not three,* Lorie thought.

At the corner of Wembly and Lorain where Melissa turned to go home, Lorie stopped. "Why don't you come over?" she asked Melissa. "Call your mom from my house the way you do sometimes."

"I told her I'd come straight home today,"

Melissa said, flinging her blond hair back. "We're having company tonight and Mom is kind of nervous about it. I have to run the vacuum and stuff."

"Doesn't your mother have cleaning help?" Karen asked.

"Yes, and I'm it." Melissa backed down the sidewalk, waving. "See you tomorrow, Lor."

"I'll call you." Lorie raised her voice. "We have to talk about—you know."

"I'll be home, slaving away," Melissa called.

"I live down Lorain, about half a block," Lorie said, turning to Karen. "And I have to get home because Mom's working today and my little brother will be into everything if I don't stop him."

"Is it all right if I walk home with you?" Karen asked, her green eyes shimmery and bright. "I'd love to meet your little brother."

"Well, okay," Lorie said as they began to walk once more. "But I can't understand why you'd want to meet my little brother. He's a brat."

Five minutes later they walked up the driveway and headed for the back door. Even before they stepped inside, Lorie could hear the television blaring away in the family room.

"Josh," Lorie shouted as they walked into the kitchen. "Turn it off. You know the rules."

Josh appeared in the doorway, his dark

blond hair standing straight up as if it were wired. "But there's going to be a show on about dinosaurs. I've *got* to see it."

"What have you got on your hair? Have you been in Mom's hair stuff again?" Lorie plopped her book bag down with a sigh.

But Josh just pointed at Karen. "Who's she?"

"This is Karen, a new girl at school," Lorie answered.

"Sounds like you love dinosaurs," Karen said, rummaging around in her purse.

Lorie tried not to groan. "That's the understatement of the twentieth century. He lives and breathes dinosaurs."

Karen fished something from her purse. "Look," she said, holding up an eraser in the shape of a brontosaurus. "It's yours if you wash that gook out of your hair."

"Terrific," Josh yelled. "I'll be right back." He raced into the hall as Lorie watched in amazement.

"Wow, Karen," Lorie said. "Do you have a little brother?"

"No," Karen said. "I just know how to handle people."

"I can see that," Lorie said, feeling a twinge of admiration. "Are you hungry? Do you want something to eat?"

"An apple or something." Karen was wandering around the kitchen, touching things. "I like your house."

"It's a real mess today." Lorie stared at the dishes in the sink, the cereal boxes still on the breakfast table, and the pile of laundry on a chair. "Mom had to work today."

"Oh, neat. Your mom has a career," Karen said. "Is she a lawyer or something?"

"No. She's a dance teacher. Mostly she teaches kids, but on Monday mornings she teaches tap dancing to a bunch of older ladies. And then she has toddlers' tap after that. Monday is a real busy day for her."

"I'll bet she's cute," Karen said, sitting down at the table and biting into her apple.

"She is," Lorie agreed, smiling. "What does your mom do?"

"Not much," Karen answered quickly. "Oh, she volunteers when there are elections. But mostly she just stays home and decorates."

"Oh." Lorie looked inside the refrigerator, wondering if she should act pleased or not since Karen didn't sound exactly thrilled about what her mom did.

Josh, his hair wet but clean, skipped back into the kitchen. "Where's my dinosaur?"

Karen handed it to him as she said, "What do you say when someone gives you something?"

24

"Thanks," Josh answered. "Thanks a lot. Hey, here comes Mr. Higby." He ran to the back door and opened it for a grandfatherly-looking man dressed in jeans and a plaid shirt. Mr. Higby was carrying a basket of vegetables. He put it on the counter near the sink.

"That's the last of the Silver Queens from my garden this year," he said, holding up several ears of corn. "But there's still plenty of tomatoes and squash."

"I hate squash," Josh said. "I wish you could plant chocolate." He began to poke around the basket.

"Josh! Have some manners!" Lorie said. "Hi, Mr. Higby. Thanks for the vegetables. This is someone I met at school. Karen, this is Mr. Higby, our next-door neighbor."

"Hello there, young lady." Mr. Higby offered his huge, wrinkled hand to shake. "Any friend of Lorie's is a friend of mine."

Wait a minute! Lorie thought. *She isn't a friend of mine yet. I just met her.*

But Karen was giving Mr. Higby a dazzling smile. "Then I know we're going to be best friends, too," she said.

Too? Lorie thought. *What does she mean by that? Don't I have anything to say about this best friend stuff?*

25

Three

THE first week of school had really gone fast, Lorie thought, despite a few complications. Now, as she walked alone to school on Monday morning, she thought about what bothered her most. First, it was this, walking alone to school without Melissa. Early band practice was taking up so much of Melissa's time that Lorie had hardly seen her since the first day of school. Well, maybe that wasn't exactly true. Lorie had finally managed to talk to Melissa about the elections one day after school. Lorie was almost as excited about nominating her best friend as Melissa was about the idea of being class president.

But they hadn't seen each other much since. Maybe that would change after Back-to-School Night when the band was scheduled to give its first performance.

Lorie sighed as she hopped over a puddle. Of

course, she could always have Karen's company.

That was the other thing Lorie worried about. Karen seemed nice enough, but she never gave a person breathing room. She was one of the cutest girls in class, she wore super neat clothes, and she could talk to anyone about anything. That was a talent to be admired. In fact, Karen could be friends with anyone she chose.

So why has she chosen me? Lorie wondered. *I'm just an average seventh grader. I'm shy, tall, and skinny. My grades are okay, but still . . . why me?*

Karen had come home with Lorie nearly every day last week, sometimes bringing a new kind of dinosaur toy for Josh. Even if Lorie didn't invite her to stay, Karen wanted to stop in. Just for a minute, she'd say. Just for a minute so I can give Josh this dinosaur whistle or pencil or whatever.

Lorie ran the rest of the way to school as it began to rain. She should have listened to her mom and worn her raincoat or at least carried her umbrella. But she hadn't, and now she was going to look like a drowned rat for the rest of the morning.

Oh, great, she thought glumly. Why today, when she had to stand up in front of her homeroom and nominate Melissa for president of seventh grade? Not that she had to—*wanted* to was more like it. It was only the getting up and talking that bothered her. But she'd do it for her best friend.

Inside, Lorie hurried to her locker and quickly dialed the combination. Then she looked in the mirror fastened to the door.

"You look like a drowned rat," Buzz said, standing beside her.

"Thanks a bunch." Lorie didn't bother to turn around.

But it was true. Her worst fears stared back at her from the mirror. She grabbed her brush from her book bag and pulled at the wet tangles on her head. It only got worse.

"Just thought you'd like to know," Buzz said, leaning against the locker next to hers.

"You could have spared me." But she smiled at Buzz because at least he was honest.

"You're in a good mood today, aren't you?" Buzz asked.

Lorie slammed her locker as she gave up on her hair. "I guess I'm just a little nervous. I'm going to nominate someone in homeroom today, and, well, you know how I am about making speeches."

Buzz stood up straight now. "So who's it going to be?"

Lorie laughed. "I'm not telling—no way! You'll just have to find out later, I guess."

She hurried on to homeroom, feeling better now. Lorie slipped into her seat and looked around. Where was Karen? She was usually here ahead of Lorie. Maybe she was sick or something. Lorie didn't want to admit it, but she felt a bit relieved. A day without Karen's attention wouldn't be too hard to take.

Lorie glanced up and noticed a new poster of a group of dogs in various sizes, colors, and breeds that Mr. Crawford had tacked above the top of the chalkboard. BE WHO YOU ARE. WHO ELSE IS BETTER QUALIFIED? it said.

Just as the tardy bell rang, Karen ran in from the hall and took her seat. "That was really close," she whispered to Lorie as Mr. Crawford went through his usual throat-clearing and began to take attendance. "My mom insisted on driving me, and she couldn't find the umbrella that matches her raincoat."

Lorie glanced back to see if Karen was kidding or serious, but she couldn't tell.

"Today, we're going to nominate class officers," Mr. Crawford began. This morning, his white bow tie had blue boats on it. "I hope your nomination speeches are ready, ladies and gentlemen. Why don't we start with nominations for student council? Who wants to be first?"

A low murmur began as kids started to whisper back and forth. There were a few giggles. But Lorie couldn't make a sound. She was too tense to even make a nervous cough. Nothing. Her mouth felt as dry as sandpaper. She couldn't speak right now if she had to! But surely, in a few minutes, after a few speeches, she'd be ready. Unless, of course, someone else nominated Melissa. Wouldn't that be great? Then she wouldn't have to do it at all. But she wanted to. She really wanted to be the one to nominate her best friend for president.

Now a boy at the back of the room stumbled his way forward and turned to face everyone. He cleared his throat and his voice squeaked as he began. Everyone laughed and that seemed to ease the tension.

"I want to nominate . . . ." His voice trailed off as Lorie only half listened. She didn't know this kid or the boy he was nominating for student council.

After he finished, others volunteered and nominated classmates for other offices.

"And now nominations are open for class president," Mr. Crawford said. He smiled and waited, tugging at his bow tie. "Come on, kids, we're running out of time."

Now, Lorie thought. *Now.* She started to raise her hand. Mr. Crawford looked in her direction. "Yes? Do you want to nominate someone?"

Lorie tried to answer, at least nod her head, but it was stuck, along with the words.

Suddenly, she heard a loud "Yes" from behind her. Then Karen rose from her seat and walked to the front of the room.

Lorie's sigh came from a well deep within her. *I'll go next,* she thought.

"The person I want to nominate for president is really special," Karen began. "She's not show-offy or smart-alecky, but just the person I'd want to be my class president. Everybody likes her because she's really nice. And she's responsible, too. I know, because I've seen her take care of her little brother and do her homework and get it in on time and never complain.

"She's a person who's easy to be around and doesn't insist on having her own way. So I'm nominating Lorie Scott for our class president!"

Karen walked down the aisle and sat down before the words really hit Lorie. They came in funny little waves, almost like ocean waves that got bigger and bigger as Lorie understood them better. As the words finally washed over her, she almost shouted, "Wait! Not me!"

But she just sat there, stunned, as Mr. Crawford's voice came through her trance. Loudly and clearly she heard, "If there aren't any more nominations, then the nominations will be closed." The bell rang.

There was a rustle of papers and notebooks as students moved out of their seats and up the aisles.

Slowly Lorie turned around to face Karen.

"Surprise," Karen said, her eyes shining. "You didn't know I was going to do that, did you?"

Lorie shook her head. "I can't run for office," she said. "I can't make speeches and all that stuff. I wouldn't know how to run a meeting even if I was elected."

"Don't worry." Karen stood up and gathered her books together. "I'll help you. Look—I'll be your campaign manager so you don't have a thing to worry about. Just leave everything to me."

Lorie had stood up and followed Karen to the door when the awful fact struck her—she hadn't nominated Melissa! Oh, no! She'd forgotten about it in her shock over Karen's move. Now what was she going to do?

Somehow Lorie made it through the

morning, through math, social studies, and Spanish. But everything blurred so that math somehow sounded like Spanish and the social studies assignment written on the chalkboard could easily have been an equation.

Now Lorie stood outside the cafeteria, waiting for Melissa. *I have to explain it to her so she'll understand,* she thought. *But maybe it will be okay because maybe someone else has nominated her.*

Buzz came bouncing down the hall first. "Hey, I hear we're going to be mortal enemies," he said.

"I don't want to play games now, Buzz," she said. "I'm busy."

"You're busy?" he asked, looking her up and down. "You're just standing there with a faraway look in your eyes and that's busy?"

"Buzz, later, okay?" Lorie didn't mean to sound cross, but right now, she couldn't stand any teasing. Suddenly she saw Melissa walking toward her.

"Melissa," Lorie shouted, running to meet her. "Melissa, I have to tell you something."

"Did you hear that Buzz has been nominated for president?" Melissa asked. "I guess that means I'll be campaigning against him!"

"I don't know," Lorie said vaguely. "Oh,

Melissa, this is awful. I can't believe it!"

"What's awful?" Melissa looked worried. "Was it hard to give the speech? I know that's not your thing."

Buzz strolled up, his hands in his pockets, his L.A. Dodgers cap far back on his head. "So did you hear the news?"

"About you?" Melissa asked. "Yeah, it's great, Buzz. But I hope you can run a clean campaign against me. No funny stuff." Melissa laughed and gave him a poke on his arm.

"Against you?" Buzz looked from Melissa to Lorie and back again. "Did I miss something?"

"What about me?" Karen, as if from nowhere, joined the group. "Have I missed something? Tell me everything."

"I think I have something to tell Melissa." Lorie spoke the words slowly and carefully.

"What is it, Lor?" Melissa began to twirl a strand of her long, blond hair.

"It's . . . well . . . ."

"Did you know I nominated Lorie for president?" Karen spoke up.

Melissa looked at Lorie.

"And I didn't . . . didn't nominate you, Melissa," Lorie said. "I got so flustered after Karen made her speech that I guess I forgot. Maybe someone else did though. Maybe someone from another homeroom nominated you."

Lorie tried to look back at Melissa but couldn't bring her eyes up from the floor.

"No, I've got the nominations right here." Karen waved a piece of paper at them. "I went to the office and got a list of all the nominations from the seventh-grade home-rooms. For president, it's Lorie and Buzz and someone named Doug Hill running against each other."

"Hey, Lorie," Buzz said. "Let's have a debate in assembly like the Democrats and Republicans do. Wouldn't that be super?"

"I'm Lorie's campaign manager, so you'll have to speak to me about that," Karen said importantly. "And I'll have to speak to your manager to arrange it. Who is it?"

"I don't know," Buzz said. "Didn't know I was supposed to have one."

"How about me?" Melissa asked, her blue eyes snapping. "I'm available."

Lorie looked up and stared at Melissa. She couldn't blame Melissa for being angry, but she didn't have to desert her and go over to the enemy camp, did she? *Oh, Melissa,* she thought. *What's happening to our friendship?*

Four

LORIE managed to slip away after school that afternoon without Karen. She didn't go back to her locker where Karen would probably be waiting. She just eased out the side doors in the hall nearest English class and hurried home through the rain. She desperately needed to talk to her parents about what had happened.

Then she remembered. It was Monday, her mom's second longest day at the studio. Mondays meant that Mom would be tired when she got home. Josh would want Mom's attention as well. And Dad? He had his newspaper and Monday night football.

Just great, Lorie thought. *Who invented Mondays anyway?* She heard the television blaring away in the family room as she opened the back door. "Josh," she yelled. "Turn it off."

She dumped her book bag on a kitchen chair and opened the refrigerator. The contents didn't look too interesting.

"Lorie."

She spun around to see Karen standing in the doorway of the family room. "Karen! How . . . ."

"Mom came to pick me up at school because of the rain. When you didn't show up at your locker, I just had Mom drop me off here. Josh let me in."

"Oh," Lorie said, staring at the carton of milk in her hand and wondering how it got there.

"I wondered if something was wrong." Karen came all the way into the kitchen now. "Why did you hurry away from school so fast?"

"It's just that . . . that I need time to think. So much has happened so fast that I have to talk it out . . . ." Before she could say that she wanted to talk to her parents, Karen interrupted.

"So . . . talk to me. I'm your friend."

"Karen, you don't understand."

"What don't I understand?"

Lorie shrugged. This was so hard. How do you tell someone you've already got a best friend, that no one else need apply for the job?

"I know that you're nervous about all this," Karen said. "But I told you to leave everything to me. You'll see, it'll be fun. Now, I've got some really terrific ideas about your campaign posters," she said. "Wait till you hear."

"Karen," Lorie said. "I have to change out of my school clothes. I'm a little wet from the rain."

"Okay, I'll come with you. I've never seen your room."

Lorie sighed, then led the way into the hall and down to her room. She opened the door to the sight of her unmade bed and a tumble of clothes piled in a chair near her desk. Oh, no! There was her plate and milk glass from her bedtime snack still in the middle of the floor.

"It's kind of messy," Lorie admitted.

"No, I think it's great," Karen said, stepping over the plate and glass and flopping down on the bed. She picked up a teen magazine that was laying beside the bed. "Oh, good. You get this magazine, too. I want to show you this girl in an ad, Lorie," she said, flipping through the pages. "Here it is. I think you should wear your hair like this. You'd really look older." Karen held up the page. "It would look more— you know—sophisticated."

"Are you kidding? I could never look like that." Lorie slipped out of her wet shoes. Did

Karen really think she could? "Besides . . . ."

"Come on, you want kids to notice you," Karen insisted. "I'll show you how to fix your hair like that. This'll be so much fun," she went on, bouncing on Lorie's bed.

"I don't know." Lorie shook her head. "If I decide to run . . . ."

"What do you mean, if you decide?" Karen stopped bouncing and ran over to stand in front of Lorie. "You *have* to run for president."

"But I don't know anything about making speeches."

"That comes later," Karen said. "First, let's get a committee together and make some posters. I met two girls in P.E. who said they'd help, and there's this boy in English . . . ."

"Is it all right if I pick some kids, too?" Lorie asked.

"Sure, I don't mind," Karen said. "But we don't have that much time, you know."

The telephone rang in the hall. "I'll get it while you're changing," Karen said as she ran into the hall.

Lorie quickly pulled off her skirt and blouse and threw them on the bed. If that was Melissa calling, she wanted to be dressed and ready to talk to her.

Karen came back in before Lorie could pull her old sweatshirt over her head. "Who was it?

Was it a wrong number?"

"No, that was Melissa," Karen answered, getting comfortable on the bed again. "Now, where were we?"

"Why didn't you tell me?"

"I just did."

"What did she say?" Lorie asked. "I'm going to call her back."

"She was just leaving, so she probably isn't there now."

Lorie felt like hitting something. Maybe it was Karen. "What did she want?"

"She said she and her mom were going to the mall and wanted to know if you wanted to come too, but guessed you couldn't because you had company."

Lorie felt like screaming now. She loved to go to the mall with Melissa and it would have been the perfect time to soothe over the little rough spot they'd had today. Now Melissa would think—well, what *would* she think?

The telephone began to ring again, and this time Lorie bolted for the door. Maybe it was Melissa calling back. "Hello," she said.

"This is Mrs. Bradley," a cool voice said. "May I speak with Karen, please?"

Lorie called Karen and went back to her room while Karen talked. When Karen returned a moment later, she didn't look happy at all. She began to gather her things.

"Mom's coming to get me now," she said. "I have to go home."

"Oh." Lorie could see by Karen's face that she didn't want to leave. But inside, Lorie was relieved.

* * * * *

The next day, Lorie felt better about everything. The idea of running for class president wasn't quite so frightening. She had even begun to think of a slogan or two. *Maybe it will be okay,* she thought, hurrying home from school, alone again. Melissa had band practice and Karen had to go somewhere with her mother.

Lorie's mom and dad were in the kitchen when she opened the back door. "Hi," Lorie said. "This is a surprise. Is everything okay?"

"Great," Mrs. Scott said. She was toweling her dark, curly hair dry. "My exercise ladies cancelled this afternoon, so I came home early."

"I ended up with an extra cook today, so I took some time off," Mr. Scott said. "I thought I'd try out a new barbequed chicken dish on my family."

"If we don't get sick, he'll try it out on his

customers." Mrs. Scott slapped her towel at him. "Now what's Josh up to?" she asked no one in particular. "He's too quiet." She went into the family room.

Lorie's father turned back to the stove, and Lorie joined him. "What is it this time, Dad? I hope it isn't too hot and spicy."

"You're in luck. No chili peppers in this sauce." He began to stir as he asked, "So what's new with you, hon?"

Lorie paused. This would be the perfect time to talk with her dad. "Well, I was nominated for president yesterday."

Dad stopped stirring and turned to look at her. "That's nice. Of what? The United States?"

"Oh, Dad, get serious. Of seventh grade."

"I think it's time you did something like that. You need to move out of your little shell. Did Melissa nominate you?"

"No, Karen did."

"That new girl who's been coming over here?" Dad asked. "Good for her! She must be a smart young lady to see your potential."

"She's smart enough, I guess."

"Have you got a campaign plan yet?" Mr. Scott asked, testing a piece of chicken with a fork.

"No, but Karen says we have to think of one

pretty soon. She's my campaign manager."

"You'll need a platform," Lorie's dad went on.

"A platform?"

"You know, some issues—things you want to accomplish while you're in office. Just listen to the TV news if you want some examples. Before long the presidential nominees will be campaigning for things like a better economy, lower taxes, more jobs. Here, Lorie, taste this."

Lorie sipped some sauce from a wooden spoon. "It needs something, Dad. Maybe more salt. What if I campaigned for a better bike rack at the side door of school? Would that be a good platform?"

"Does the school need a better bike rack there?"

"It sure does. The one we've got now is too small and too rickety. I heard some kids talking about it during homeroom."

"How much would a new one cost?"

"I don't know." Lorie shrugged.

"Then you'd better find out so you can answer that question when someone asks."

Lorie frowned. "I wonder if I can handle this."

"You'll never know till you try," Dad answered.

"Right." Lorie nodded. "That's right. You know what I'm going to do? I'm going to call my committee over right now so we can make posters and stuff. Oh, and Dad . . . please promise you won't make them taste anything."

Lorie called the names that Karen had given her, and a little while later, two girls knocked at her door. Sandy was from her old sixth grade class at Weston, and April was in some of Lorie's classes.

"This is so much fun," Sandy said. "I like being involved in things right away."

April spoke up. "Where's Karen? Do you think we should start without her?"

Lorie tried not to sound irritated. "Why not? My name's going to be the one on the posters. Anyway, I found some poster paints in the basement, so we can get started right away."

Lorie began to have fun as they thought of poster ideas and put them on paper. An hour later, five completed posters sat around the room, drying. "They're good," Lorie said. She looked at her campaign slogan, Vote for Lorie, printed across the top of each one.

"I think you ought to put your school pictures on the posters," April said. "You have extras, don't you?"

"Good idea," Lori agreed. "I'll look in my desk tonight. Can you come back tomorrow?

I'll need more help," Lorie said.

"Sure," Sandy said, standing up. "When can we put these posters up?"

"First thing in the morning . . . if that's okay with you. I'll meet you by the big bulletin board near the cafeteria."

The telephone rang as the girls were leaving. "Go ahead," April said. "Maybe it's a boy."

"Fat chance," Lorie said, laughing. She didn't know a boy who'd call her unless it was good old Buzz. But now she doubted that he'd be calling.

"Hi, Lorie." It was Karen. "I'm sorry I couldn't make it today, but maybe we can get together tomorrow and make posters. I bought tons of supplies, paint, paper, colored markers—everything."

"Karen . . ." Lorie hesitated. Suddenly she felt as if she needed to apologize. But why? Why did Karen make her feel like an intruder in her own campaign? "Sandy and April came over and we made a few posters today."

"Without me?" Karen wailed. "I should have been there."

"We only made five," Lorie said, apologizing again. "You can help us put them up tomorrow."

"Okay, but I get to help with everything else from now on. Hey, guess what?" Karen's voice suddenly switched from mad to happy.

"What?"

"I had to go with Mom to the store today."

"And . . . ?" Lorie couldn't imagine what this had to do with her.

"Well, while we were at the store, I got something."

"A new dress?"

"No, it isn't for me. It's for you."

"Me?" Lorie couldn't figure out what Karen was talking about. "I give up. You'll have to tell me."

"Tomorrow. I'll show you tomorrow after we put up the posters."

Five

THE following morning, Lorie was still puzzled by Karen's announcement. *What does Karen have to give me?* Lorie wondered, hurrying down Lorain Road. She slowed to pull her sweater collar up around her throat. After yesterday's rain, the weather had turned cooler and the slight wind had a damp, biting edge to it.

Why a present? she continued to wonder. The kids at school didn't exchange gifts, except on birthdays when there were parties. She and Melissa exchanged Christmas presents, but that's because they were best friends.

So what was going on with Karen? Lorie was kind of excited to think she might be getting a present for no reason at all. But did that mean she had to give one back? And where would she get the money? Her allowance wasn't anything to brag about.

As Lorie turned the corner at the end of her block, she saw Melissa walking along Wembly. Melissa slowed down when she saw Lorie. Lorie slowed too, feeling strange and different, but wanting everything to be the same as before.

"Hi, Lorie," Melissa said, shifting her books and trombone case from one arm to the other. "I . . . I'm surprised to find you alone."

"Oh, you mean where's Karen?"

"She seems to be around so much lately." Melissa hesitated as if searching for the right words. "I just assumed she'd be walking with you from now on."

"Her mother's been driving her the last couple of days, with the bad weather and all."

Melissa and Lorie began to walk together. "Why don't they stop and pick you up? Karen said she lives out in our area, so it wouldn't be out of their way."

"Well, it's sort of out in this direction." Lorie had wondered that, too, until Karen explained where she really lived. "Karen's folks bought a house in that new development, Upper Ridgecrest."

"Oh, wow," breathed Melissa. "You mean where all those huge houses are? I'll bet they've got a gorgeous place. What's Karen's room like? I'll bet it's gorgeous."

"She hasn't invited me yet. She says her mom is redecorating."

"Really?" Melissa raised her eyebrows in disbelief.

Lorie nodded. "And get this. She likes to come to my house all the time. Can you believe it? I think she's crazy to like dishes in the sink and a kid brother whose middle name is Messy."

Melissa shrugged. "I just figured you'd gone to her house by now." They walked on without speaking for a few minutes.

"What's in that big sack?" Melissa asked finally, eyeing the package Lorie carried.

"Five campaign posters. I'm going to put them up at school this morning."

"I wondered why you were going to school so much earlier than usual."

"What about you?" Lorie eyed Melissa's trombone case. "Band practice again?"

Melissa laughed. "Not until after school. This morning I'm meeting with Buzz and some other kids to put up campaign stuff around school, too."

"I wish . . . " Lorie began. "I wish . . . ."

"I know," Melissa sighed. "I wish we were working together, too. I don't know how all of this happened."

"It was my fault," Lorie said. "I got so distracted when Karen nominated me that I couldn't think straight. I should have jumped up, refused the nomination, and then nominated you."

"But you've got as much right to be president as anyone else," Melissa said.

"It's nice to hear you say that." Lorie sighed.

"Next year we'll be on the same team no matter what happens," Melissa said.

"You can count on it."

Then they ran the rest of the way to school as it began to rain again.

Lorie met Sandy and April, and they quickly put up the five posters around school. Karen didn't appear until Lorie was already in homeroom.

"I'm late again," Karen said, sliding into her seat as the tardy bell rang. "But I saw one of your posters when I went to my locker."

"And?" Lorie waited. "What did you think of it?"

"It's okay," Karen said. "Especially for your first try."

Lorie didn't know if that was a compliment or not.

Karen whispered now, looking at Mr. Crawford as he stood up to make some announcements. "Anyway, look what I brought you."

Lorie turned around quickly to see a brightly wrapped package in Karen's hands. "What is it?" she whispered. She felt a rush of excitement.

"Go ahead and find out," Karen whispered back.

Lorie took the small package in her hands and turned around to face the front of the room. It felt light. She wanted to shake it to see if it rattled. Did she dare open it now?

Lorie looked up at the sudden silence in the room. Mr. Crawford stared at her and cleared his throat.

"Is it your birthday, Lorie?" Mr. Crawford asked.

"No." She felt her face begin to redden.

"Maybe it's a bribe to throw the election," a boy's voice called from the back of the room.

Everyone laughed. Lorie wanted to sink out of sight beneath her desk. Quickly she put the gift under her seat, opened her notebook to a blank page and stared at it. She wanted to die of embarrassment.

"Okay, everyone," Mr. Crawford said. "Back to the announcements."

As soon as the bell rang ending homeroom, Lorie turned around. "I can't accept this,

Karen," she began. "There's no reason for it."

"There doesn't have to be, silly," Karen said, standing up. "I want you to have it."

"But I can't. I can't just take a present like this."

"It's a friendship present. Can't a friend give another friend a present? What's the big deal anyway?" A frown appeared on Karen's forehead and she walked up the aisle toward the door.

Lorie gathered up her things and moved to the exit. Mr. Crawford stood beside the door. He smiled as Lorie walked past. "How's the campaign going, Lorie?"

"Okay."

"Got someone to help you?"

"Uh, yes . . . Karen. She's a big help."

"Well, that's great. Good luck to you!" Mr. Crawford stepped back to the chalkboard.

"Thanks, Mr. Crawford." Lorie rushed into the hall, hoping to catch Karen before the first period. But she'd disappeared and was probably already in class. Since Karen sat across the room from Lorie in math, there'd be no chance to talk now.

Karen avoided Lorie all morning as they moved from one class to another. At noon, before she went to the cafeteria, Lorie put the unopened package on the shelf of her locker, wondering what to do with it. It was so tempting to untie the blue bow and tear the bright paper off the box. Would it be okay to open it and see what it was before handing it back? No, that wouldn't be right. Lorie sighed. It was so hard to know how to handle this. New experiences were happening right and left since she started junior high. What was the rest of the year going to be like?

* * * * *

Lorie found Karen sitting with Sandy and April at a cafeteria table. She put her tray down and pulled up a chair. "Can you come over to my house and make some more posters this afternoon?" Lorie asked.

"Okay, but let's think up something that's jazzier this time," Karen said. "Wait'll you see the new markers I bought."

"What's the matter with the posters we put up this morning?" Sandy asked. "I think they look great. Don't you, Lorie?"

"Well," Lorie hesitated. "Karen thought—"

"You know what?" Karen interrupted. "I just thought of something. The window trimmer down at the store could help us. He's terrific with posters and slogans and things. Wait till you see the storewide clearance display he just put up at The Best."

"Karen, this is a school election, not a store sale," April said.

"But elections are like sales," Karen said. "And what we have to sell is Lorie."

"I don't know . . . ." Lorie poked at the food on her plate.

"Karen's got a point," April went on. "Look at the way the governors and senators do it in their campaigns. They have ads in all the newspapers, ads on television. If that isn't selling, I don't know what is."

Karen took over the conversation. Sandy and April contributed now and then, while Lorie listened and waited for a chance to talk. Should she just interrupt the way they were interrupting one another? After all, it was her campaign.

"Karen," she began.

But no one seemed to hear. Suddenly she looked up to see Melissa looking at her from another table. How long had she been watching?

The afternoon moved slowly for Lorie. She couldn't concentrate on her subjects at all. Instead her mind moved from the gift in her locker to her campaign slogans and back to the gift again. First, what was in the box? Then, what new slogan could she think of that was better than Vote for Lorie?

Finally the bell ended the last class of the day. Lorie hurried to her locker, wondering if Karen would be there, waiting. What would she say if Karen spotted the unopened gift in Lorie's locker?

Sure enough, there she was. "Hi, Karen," Lorie began, feeling tense and uncertain.

"Lorie, I just wanted to tell you that I'm going to get some more coloring pencils at the drugstore and then I'll be over. I won't be long. Sandy and April said they'd get more paper."

Lorie waited until Karen had disappeared down the corridor before she breathed a deep sigh and opened her locker. There sat the unopened present.

Lorie couldn't stand it any longer. She had to know what was inside. She picked up the package and ripped the paper from it. Inside, she found a box embossed The Best Department Store on the lid.

Carefully she removed the lid from the box and pushed away white tissue paper. She lifted out a hair barrette—not just any barrette, but one heavy with glittery, shiny rhinestones covering it. But she couldn't wear this! Maybe *Karen* would . . . after all, she bought it. But it was way too sophisticated for Lorie's taste. Why had Karen bought this for her anyway?

"Are those real diamonds?"

Lorie nearly dropped the barrette as she whirled around. "Of course not. Buzz, why don't you wear a bell?"

"So, who's the present from?" Buzz ignored her blast and leaned against the locker next to hers. "Have you got a boyfriend?"

Lorie began to put the barrette back in the box. "Don't be silly. It's . . . it's from a friend. A plain friend."

"A rich friend," he corrected.

Lorie glanced up, wondering if he knew it was from Karen. But if he did, his face gave nothing away. "See you," he said as he tipped his Dodgers cap and walked away.

Lorie met Melissa at their corner the next morning and they headed for school. This time, Melissa carried campaign posters for Buzz.

"We had so much fun making these posters last night," Melissa began. "Buzz kept cutting up. You should have heard some of the slogans we didn't use."

"Oh, tell me," Lorie begged. "I can just imagine."

"I can't repeat a single one," Melissa said, acting mysterious. "We may use some of them later."

Lorie felt a stab of envy. She knew Melissa

and Buzz would have fun working on their posters. Why couldn't it be that way with her committee? Why did Karen have to be so serious and bossy? Somehow, last night's meeting had seemed totally grim.

"Tell me about your campaign," Melissa said. "How's it going?"

"Well, if I weren't so scared, maybe I'd enjoy it more," Lorie began. "But you know me. I'm really trying though, to think about my campaign platform, stuff like that."

"What's it going to be?" Melissa asked.

"That's a big secret so far," Lorie answered. "And besides, you're the enemy, remember?"

"You're going to have to tell pretty soon." Melissa paused to change her posters from one arm to the other. "Don't forget about the assembly next week when all the candidates have to give a talk."

"Don't remind me." Lorie felt her stomach knot up at the thought.

They opened the doors to the main hall and went inside. "I have to meet Buzz now," Melissa said. "See you at lunch."

Lorie waved and moved along to the hall where her locker was located. On the way, she decided to detour and walk past the big display board by the cafeteria to look at her poster. So what if Karen said it wouldn't bring in any votes? Karen didn't know everything.

A group of kids stood around the display boards as she walked up. Lorie wondered what the attraction could be. Had Buzz put up some of his own posters already?

Then she saw it. It was her poster, with Vote for Lorie printed across the top. Only someone had scrawled above it a big "Don't." But that wasn't all. On her school picture, someone had drawn a mustache.

Six

"YOU should have seen the posters this morning, Mom," Lorie said. She was setting the table for supper while her mom stirred something in a pan on the stove. "I had to throw them away. They looked so terrible, and everyone was laughing at them. I wanted to die on the spot."

"I wish I could have seen the posters," Josh piped up, trying to fold napkins. "I would have died laughing."

"Oh, Josh," Lorie glared at him. "You're rotten. Say you're sorry."

"What have I got to be sorry about?" He shrugged and dropped all the napkins on the floor.

"Mom . . . ." Lorie's voice took off in a wail.

"Joshua," Mom said. "This is important to your sister. She's running for class president and someone has defaced her posters."

"Defaced?" Josh looked at his mom in total innocence. "Does that mean drawing pictures on de face?" Then he darted out of the kitchen as Lorie made a grab for him.

Lorie looked at her mom, who in turn looked at her. Mrs. Scott's mouth began to twitch as she tried to hide a giggle. Lorie couldn't help herself and began to smile, too.

"Wrong choice of words, honey," her mom said. "Sorry."

"It's okay." Lorie sighed. "I suppose I should be a good sport about it. But it's hard."

"Of course it is." Mrs. Scott took a casserole out of the oven. "It was really cruel of someone to do that."

"Or else someone has a weird idea of what's funny," Lorie said. "I'm trying to figure out who did it."

"That's easy," Josh said, deciding it was safe to come back. He began picking up the napkins he'd dropped. "It's your enemy."

"Buzz, or Doug Hill?" Lorie stared at Josh while she thought. "I don't even know Doug, but I do know Buzz and his weird sense of humor. I'm going to call him right now."

"After we eat," her mom said. "The food is hot and we're not waiting for Dad tonight. He has to work late."

Lorie ate quickly, hardly tasting the tuna

60

casserole or the broccoli from Mr. Higby's garden. As soon as she gulped down the last of her milk, she asked to be excused and hurried to the phone in the hall. She dialed Buzz's number and waited. His mother answered on the fourth ring.

"Hi, Mrs. Howard," Lorie said. "May I speak to Buzz, please?"

"He's eating, Lorie," she said. "I'll have him call you back when he's finished. But that may be hours, honey. You know how much he eats these days." She laughed.

Lorie politely laughed with Mrs. Howard, but it wasn't easy. Then she hung up.

Before she could get too far from the telephone, it rang. "Hello," Lorie answered.

"Hi," Karen said. "Have you finished dinner? Can I come over so we can work on some new posters?"

"I'm not sure I want to."

"Why?" Karen demanded. "Just because someone had a little fun?"

"Maybe you wouldn't feel that way if your face had a mustache drawn on it."

There was a slight pause before Karen said, "Well, maybe not. But this time we'll make posters that can't be so easily changed."

There she goes again, Lorie thought, *Miss Know-It-All.*

"Do you know who did it?" Karen asked.

"I've got ideas," Lorie answered. "I'll probably never be able to prove it though."

"Buzz, you mean."

"Well, maybe." Lorie hated to come right out and say it. Buzz was an old friend, wasn't he?

"Or someone working to get Buzz elected," Karen said.

Lorie knew who she meant. Melissa. Karen meant Melissa. "No way," she answered aloud. "There's no way Melissa would do anything like that to hurt me."

"You never can be too sure about people," Karen said. "I'll see you in a little while."

Lorie walked back into the kitchen and began to stare out the window that faced Mr. Higby's house. Over the fence that separated their yards, she could see the top of his gardening hat moving up and down the rows of vegetables. Although it was nearly dark, he was still out there working. He was probably picking something that he'd bring over to them. At least half of his garden's vegetables wound up on their table.

Lorie's mom came over, took Lorie's hand, and placed a dish towel in it.

"Come on, give me a hand with the dishes so I can get on with my choreography for the dance recital," her mother said.

"Dance recital?" Lorie walked over to the sink and began to dry a dinner plate. "When did you decide to let your students loose in public again?"

"This afternoon. My kids are looking pretty good." Her mom backed away from the counter. "See what you think of this routine." She began to hum to herself while she danced out some tap steps that ended in a shuffle-off-to-Buffalo.

"Looks good, Mom," Lorie said. "Except I think you ought to put in a double-time step right there." Lorie showed her mom what she meant.

"That's great, Lor," Mrs. Scott said. "Now how about three falling-off-the-log steps next?" She demonstrated the beginning sequence. Lorie joined in on the time steps.

"You always were my best student," Lorie's mom said, giving her a hug. "Now . . . I'll put on the music and we'll try it together from the top."

Mrs. Scott ran into the family room and a moment later, Lorie heard the music begin. Then she heard her mother's footsteps run down the hall to the bedrooms. Lorie knew her mom was gathering their tap shoes from their closets.

Lorie smiled. She enjoyed dancing and loved to help her mom plan the routines the little kids would perform in the recital.

Mrs. Scott was back in seconds, and they quickly put their dancing shoes on. Lorie and her mother began to tap in time with the music. Josh stood in the doorway of the family room to watch.

When the record ended, Mrs. Scott hurried into the family room to change it while Lorie kept trying new combinations.

"Come on, Josh, follow me," Lorie said.

"I don't have any tap shoes," he said.

"Silly. You don't need any. Come on, just keep time."

Her mom came back and they began to dance together again. Josh knew most of the steps already. "Maybe we ought to try out for a Broadway show," Lorie called out over the music.

As the music ended, they all took great sweeping bows to an imaginary audience. Then Lorie saw a sudden movement through the window on the back door. "Hey! Who's there?" she yelled, running to the door and opening it.

Karen stood on the porch. "Karen," Lorie said. "Why didn't you knock?"

Karen stepped inside and looked at each of

them. "You were having so much fun," she said. "I didn't want to interrupt."

"Next time don't wait for an invitation." Lorie's mom smiled. "Excuse me, I've got to put that routine down on paper before I forget it."

Josh followed his mom out of the room. "Mom, can I watch a movie on TV tonight?"

Lorie put dishes away in the cupboard. "As soon as I'm through, we can go in and start on the posters."

"You and your mom seem to have a lot of fun together," Karen said, handing Lorie a plate. "That's so different."

Lorie turned to look at her. "It is?"

"Well, you know." Karen began to trace lines on the kitchen counter. "Most girls I know fight with their mothers."

Lorie's mind ran down a list of girls' names from school. Melissa was at the top, but she never fought with her mom. Lorie knew that for a fact. No one else seemed to have mom troubles except Sandy, when she wanted to wear lipstick and her mom said no.

Lorie and Karen managed to finish a couple of posters before Karen had to go home. But it wasn't easy. Karen wanted everything her own way, and usually Lorie just gave up.

*   *   *   *   *

As she walked to school the next morning, Lorie looked for Melissa before remembering that Melissa had an extra band practice. She was probably at school already, tooting away on her trombone.

Lorie turned onto the path that led through the baseball diamond, deciding to go through the back entrance of school this morning. She glanced up to see Buzz and some of his buddies playing catch near homeplate. *Why didn't he call back last night?* she suddenly wondered. *Was it because of a guilty conscience?*

"Hey, Lorie, wait a minute." Buzz had seen her now and ambled across the diamond.

"Mom said you called last night," he began as he came closer. "But Dad wouldn't let me use the telephone until I finished all my math problems."

"Guess you didn't get finished," Lorie said, trying not to sound angry.

"Not until 9:30." Buzz said. "So what's on your mind?" He pushed his Dodgers cap back.

Lorie hesitated. How did you come right out and accuse a friend of hurting you? This wasn't going to be easy.

"It's about my posters," Lorie began. "Did you see them yesterday?"

"Yeah, and it was rotten of someone to do that." Buzz shook his head.

His reaction surprised Lorie somehow. "That's how I felt," she said. "It was so . . . so personal."

"I know," Buzz said. "I can imagine how you must feel." He opened the door for her and they walked to their lockers.

Lorie took a deep breath. "I don't suppose you've heard . . . you know, who might have done it?"

"Why would I have heard?" Buzz leaned against the locker next to hers while she dialed her combination.

"Well, you're running against me and all . . ." Lorie began. "I thought you might know something."

Buzz stood up straight and looked at her hard. "Look, if you're wondering, Lorie, I didn't do it."

Lorie felt as if she'd been stung. Buzz was an old friend and she'd practically come right out and accused him.

"Who would want to win like that?" he asked. "Besides, I've got an alibi. Those posters were defaced yesterday morning before school started, right?"

Lorie nodded.

"I had to go to the dentist first thing

yesterday morning, so I had an absence from homeroom." He paused. "You'll have to pick on someone else, Lorie." Buzz turned on his heel and walked away.

Lorie leaned against her locker door and watched him go down the hall. Just then, Karen ran up, breathless and excited.

"I saw you talking to Buzz," she said. "What did he say?"

"He said he didn't have anything to do with my posters and I believe him. Even without his excuse."

"What excuse?"

Quickly Lorie filled her in about the dental appointment.

"I guess that's airtight, isn't it?" Karen said, looking at Buzz far down the corridor. "So, as far as I'm concerned, it leaves only one other person."

Seven

BRIGHT sunshine woke Lorie on Saturday morning. She dressed quickly and hurried into the kitchen for breakfast. Mrs. Scott, dressed in a purple leotard and tights (her Saturday uniform, she called it), was flipping French toast at the stove.

"Oh, hi, hon," she said, her face brightening when she saw Lorie. "I'm so late. Can you take over for me? The little girls in my first class are always early. I've got to run."

Lorie took the spatula from her mom's hand and peeked under the pieces of toast browning on the griddle. "Mom, I need to talk to you."

"Right now?" her mom asked. She poured herself a glass of orange juice and sipped it using one hand, while she set the table with the other. "Can you wait until I get home this afternoon, hon?"

"Well, it's pretty important." Lorie flipped

two pieces of toast. "Karen said something about Melissa and. . . ."

Josh raced into the kitchen, wearing wrinkled Superman pajamas. "I smell French toast. Mom, why are you letting her cook it?" He pointed at Lorie.

"Now, Josh," Mrs. Scott began. "Lorie does a good job, you know that." She picked up her tote bag and purse from a chair. "I'm sorry, I just have to go. I'll talk to you tonight, Lorie. I really will."

Lorie sighed. "Okay." Tonight would be better than nothing, but right now, this minute, would have been best. What if Melissa called this morning and wanted to go to the mall or something? What should she do? "Josh, go tell Dad that breakfast is ready."

"Do I have to?"

"Yes, you do. Now go on." Lorie's voice sounded shrill, even to her.

"You don't have to get so mad," Josh said, hurrying out the back door.

Moments later Mr. Scott came in and washed his hands at the sink, while Josh sat down at the table and began to eat.

"Josh tells me you yelled at him," Lorie's dad said, drying his hands.

Lorie turned around and handed him a plate of toast. "I'm just . . . I'm just upset about something, that's all. Sorry, Josh, I didn't mean to take it out on you."

Her dad gave her a hug. "That was nice, sweetheart. Is it something you can talk to your old dad about? I've got time. I'm actually staying home until noon today."

"It's about Melissa," Lorie said in a rush, the words eager to jump out. She brought her own plate to the table and sat down.

"I like Melissa," Josh said. "She smells like bubble gum."

Mr. Scott laughed. "That's an endorsement if I've ever heard one. So what's with you and Melissa, Lorie? Having a best-friend spat?"

"No . . . I mean, I don't think so." Lorie paused, then plunged into an explanation of the mix-up in nominations, the defacing of the posters, and finally, Karen's accusation of Melissa.

"What do you think?" Lorie's dad asked when she had finished. "Do you really think Melissa would be involved in anything like that?"

Lorie stared at her uneaten breakfast. No, she couldn't really believe that Melissa would stoop to anything that low. But Karen made it seem so . . . so logical.

"Of course you don't." Her dad spoke for her. "Melissa is a good friend."

"The best," Lorie added.

"So don't believe what others have said. Believe in your friendship instead." Mr. Scott patted her hand.

Lorie listened and understood that her dad was right. What had she been thinking of to doubt Melissa for a second?

"Tell you what," her dad said, standing up and carrying his dishes to the sink. "Why don't you invite Melissa to my place for lunch today? It'll be my treat."

Lorie laughed. It was always her father's treat when they went. "Okay! I'll call her right away. Thanks a lot, Dad."

"Can I go, too?" Josh asked.

"You have to stay home and help clean the garage," Mr. Scott said. "I pay top prices, in case you haven't heard."

"Oh, boy," Josh said. "Let's go."

"After you put on your working clothes," his dad said. "Come on, I'll help you so we can get started." Mr. Scott took Josh by the hand and they hurried into the hall.

Lorie rinsed the breakfast dishes and stacked them in the sink for later. Right now she had more important things to do, like call Melissa.

* * * * *

By 10:30, Lorie and Melissa were walking downtown. As they passed the school, Lorie thought how easy it would be for anyone to walk inside and draw funny faces on the posters. Anyone could do it, even someone from another school. Unless the doors were locked.

"Melissa," Lorie said. "If I forgot something in my locker, could I just go in right now and get it? I still don't know all the rules for junior high."

"I don't think so," Melissa said. "Aren't the doors always locked on weekends and after 5:00 during the week?"

Lorie studied Melissa's face for a second. "Let's find out." Quickly they walked up the sidewalk to the side entrance and tried the doors. They were tightly closed. "You're right."

She peered inside and saw a custodian walk into a room at the other end of the hall. "But what if you forgot something you absolutely had to have? Do you think one of the custodians would open a door for you?"

Melissa shrugged as they began to walk toward town again. "I doubt it, but I'm not sure. Probably they're not allowed. At least, that would be my guess."

"You're probably right," Lorie said. "Maybe you could ask your neighbor, Bob."

"I'll do that." They walked for a few minutes until Melissa said, "You're still bugged by what happened to your posters, aren't you?"

"Yes." Lorie nodded.

"You can get in before school starts in the morning," Melissa said. "The teachers come early and so does the band, some mornings, remember?"

Lorie glanced at Melissa, then looked away. That suspicious little thought jumped into Lorie's mind again. Why wouldn't it go away?

"Let's go somewhere else before we go to your dad's place," Melissa said.

"Okay," Lorie agreed. "Where do you want to go?"

"To The Best." Melissa pulled a piece of paper from her pocket. "I saw these jackets advertised in the paper this morning. Don't you think they're totally gorgeous?"

"Oh, wow," Lorie said. "But they're so expensive. I don't think my mom would let me have one."

"I dön't think I could buy one either," Melissa said. "But who says we can't try one on?"

Both girls giggled. *The best times are always with Melissa,* Lorie thought.

They walked into The Best Department

Store a few minutes later, and were met by the flowery scents of the perfumes and lotions from the cosmetic department.

"Oh, isn't it wonderful?" Melissa breathed. "Let's try some of the testers."

"Okay," Lorie said, breathing deeply. She picked up a bottle labeled Bright Star and sprayed herself generously on one wrist.

"You smell good," Melissa said. "But I think this one's better." She doused herself with First Date before spraying Lorie's other arm.

They tried several more samples, glancing from time to time at the clerk who was standing at the other end of the counter. She didn't seem to mind that they were sampling, however, and continued her conversation with another clerk. Suddenly both clerks looked up and tried to act busy.

"Melissa, Lorie, hi. Try this one next."

Lorie turned around to see Karen standing behind them next to a beautiful woman wearing an elegant suit and lots of jewelry. And Karen was wearing the jacket that had been advertised in the morning newspaper.

Karen held out a tester to Lorie. "You'll love this one."

Lorie was suddenly aware of how she must smell from all the perfume. "Hi, Karen," she said. "I think I'll skip trying that one."

"I love your jacket, Karen," Melissa said.

"You should introduce me to your friends, Karen," the woman said.

"Oh, sorry," Karen began. "This is my mom, Mrs. Bradley. And this is Lorie and this is Melissa."

"Hello," Mrs. Bradley said, smiling. "I've finally met you, Lorie. Karen talks about you all the time, you know, and I've asked her to invite you over sometime. You, too, Melissa."

Lorie looked at Karen but she glanced away. So why didn't Karen invite them over then? Her mom just said it was okay.

"It's just that we've been so busy with the election," Karen said. "There hasn't been time."

"Of course," Mrs. Bradley said. "And we've been busy decorating our new house." Mrs. Bradley smiled again. "Which reminds me. We must meet the decorator right now, so we'd better go."

"Oh, can't I stay with them, Mom? Please?"

"Come along, dear." Mrs. Bradley's tone of voice was firm but she smiled directly at Lorie and Melissa. "And girls, perhaps you've tried enough perfume samples now. I think you'd better leave some for the other customers."

Karen followed her mother to the escalator

after a long, backward glance.

Lorie and Melissa wandered over to the shoe department and examined several pairs of tennis shoes. "Her mother sure has a nice smile, doesn't she?" Lorie asked.

"Pretty teeth, too," Melissa added.

Lorie nodded, wondering why Mrs. Bradley didn't seem friendly even with all that smiling. "Do you still want to try that jacket on?" she asked.

"No," Melissa said, wrinkling up the newspaper ad. "I've decided I don't want to."

"Me, neither." Lorie shoved her hands deep in the pockets of the jacket she was wearing. "But it's too early for lunch. What'll we do?"

Melissa shrugged. "I'm out of ideas. You think of something."

"We could go over to the dime store," Lorie suggested. "That's more my style anyway."

They walked over to Vanderbilt's Variety and looked at nail polish, deciding on their favorite colors. Then they moved on to hair products.

"Look, Lorie, this barrette would be perfect for you now that you've changed your hairstyle. Did I tell you I just love it pulled back like that?"

"Thanks, Melissa." Lorie didn't mention it was Karen's idea. "Do you think this style makes me look older?"

"Oh, definitely. You could pass for an eighth grader."

"Maybe I will buy this barrette," Lorie said. It was made of lightweight, reddish brown plastic, nearly matching the color of her hair. What she liked best about it was its shape. It looked like a butterfly ready to land.

As she paid for the barrette at the checkout, Lorie remembered the barrette Karen had given her. *I can't wear it,* she thought. *But what'll I do when she asks me where it is?*

"Come on, Lorie." Melissa was tugging at her sleeve. "I'm starving."

Eight

LORIE dashed into school on Monday morning, knowing she was terribly late. *Why did everything have to go wrong this morning?* she thought, dialing her locker combination and missing the last two numbers. First, Josh couldn't find his book bag. They'd had to turn the house upside down looking for it. Because they were all so busy looking for Josh's things, the bacon had burned. Then, when the kitchen filled up with smoke, the smoke alarm went off.

Lorie drew in a deep breath and started her combination once more. If she couldn't get it right this time, she'd have to go to homeroom and come back later for her books.

"It's no wonder you're late." Buzz appeared beside her, hands in his pockets. "After the busy morning you've had."

Lorie's combination clicked open and she

sighed. "How did you know?"

"Couldn't miss it." Buzz sounded serious and his usual grin was missing.

"Buzz, I don't know what you're talking about." Lorie slammed her locker door shut. "The tardy bell's about to ring. Can we talk some other time about what's bugging you?" She reached up and gave his Dodgers cap a yank.

Buzz took a step backward and frowned as the first tardy bell rang. "I'll see you at lunch." He hurried down the hall and Lorie, after a backward glance, ran toward homeroom. Was the planet turning in the right orbit today?

She slid into her seat after the last bell rang, smiling at Karen behind her.

"I'm glad you could make it, Lorie," Mr. Crawford said. Then he began the announcements, tugging on his white bow tie with the boats on it.

Lorie looked at her books to see if she had the right ones for morning classes. The way things were going, she might even have some of Josh's.

Karen touched her on the shoulder and Lorie leaned back. "Where were you?" Karen whispered.

Lorie shrugged. The explanation was too long to be whispered. But Karen didn't wait.

"Did you see Buzz's posters?" she whispered again. "They're awful, as in great."

Suddenly Lorie's conversation with Buzz made sense. He'd been accusing her of something. But what? Marking up his posters? She turned around quickly to stare at Karen. Karen was smiling, her eyes full of mischief.

"Eyes front, please." Mr. Crawford's voice was a cool reminder and Lorie turned around quickly. Her mind raced in every direction, trying to remember what Buzz had said. *No wonder you're late after your busy morning,* he'd said. Something had happened to his posters—and he thought she'd done it. Oh, no! If Buzz thought so, did Melissa think the same thing? But how could they? They were all supposed to be friends!

The bell for first period snapped Lorie out of herself and she jumped, causing everyone around her to laugh. She stood up and hurried to the door at the front of the room.

"Lorie," Mr. Crawford called.

She turned to face him. "Yes, sir?"

"You're to report to the principal's office just before lunch period. Here's your note and your pass for the hall monitors."

Lorie took the papers and stuffed them in her purse without looking up at him. Now what?

Mr. Crawford cleared his throat. "What's going on, Lorie?" he asked, puzzled.

"I'm not sure."

"Let's not be late again, okay?" he said.

"I'll remember," she said quickly, racing out the door.

"Lorie, wait." Karen hurried up beside her and they walked quickly to their first class. "What was that about, with Mr. Crawford, I mean?"

"The principal wants to see me. I just don't know what's going on." They turned from the main corridor into a smaller one. "What *is* going on, Karen? What did you mean about Buzz's posters?"

"See for yourself." Karen pointed at the bulletin board near the cafeteria.

Lorie looked and gasped. Buzz's picture had a scraggly beard drawn on it and the words *Buzz is a bum* written across the bottom. "That's just awful," Lorie managed to say. "Who would do that?"

"Guess that's what the principal wants to find out." Karen paused, then added, "Hey, maybe I'd better come to this meeting. I'm your campaign manager."

"You mean you actually *want* to go to Mrs. Lope's office? She's pretty strict, in case you haven't heard."

"Who's afraid of some junior-high-school principal?" Karen laughed. "Not me."

"Well, I'm the one who's going and I'm the one who's scared. I'll be glad when this thing is over."

"Not me," Karen said again. "I think it's great."

Lorie couldn't believe her. Being in trouble was definitely not great.

* * * * *

Lorie was excused a few minutes early from her class before lunch and hurried down the hall for her meeting with Mrs. Lope. There was Buzz, waiting in the main office with the school secretaries. Lorie sat down beside him.

"Bet you're hungry, aren't you?" Lorie whispered.

"I lost my appetite," Buzz said. "I don't like this."

"Same here," Lorie whispered.

"Buzz, Lorie, you can go in now." One of the secretaries pointed to the door leading to Mrs. Lope's private office.

Lorie followed Buzz inside and glanced around while they waited for Mrs. Lope to finish a telephone conversation.

Mrs. Lope put down the telephone and

glanced up at them, her dark eyes warm and bright. "Let's have a little chat, shall we?" She pointed to two chairs in front of the desk and waited while they sat down.

"From what I can tell by the school records, you two have known each other a long time," Mrs. Lope began.

Lorie nodded as Buzz said, "Yeah, since first grade."

"Have you had any fights or misunderstandings before?" Mrs. Lope pushed a wisp of dark hair away from her face.

Lorie shook her head. "Just the usual stuff when we were little."

"Such as?" Mrs. Lope waited.

"Like, once I threw Lorie's doll in the bushes." Buzz smiled as he remembered.

"So I hid his baseball glove in the garage," Lorie said. "Then I couldn't remember what I did with it."

Mrs. Lope looked at some papers on her desk. "You two are practically next-door neighbors, I see."

"Most of our lives," Buzz said.

"Tell me then." Mrs. Lope looked from one of them to the other. "What's happened here at school? Why are you being so difficult with one another over this election?"

Lorie looked at Buzz and he stared back.

Finally Lorie spoke. "I don't know, Mrs. Lope. I didn't touch Buzz's posters and he says he didn't touch mine. What about Doug Hill? Maybe he's involved in this."

"Oh, you haven't heard then," Mrs. Lope said. "He decided not to run. He wants to work on the school newspaper instead."

"Oh," was all Buzz said as he adjusted his book bag on his lap. "Back to what you said, Lor. I told you I had to go to the dentist that day and couldn't have drawn all that stuff on your face. Besides, it wasn't very good. You know I can draw better than that."

Mrs. Lope smiled before she spoke. "Okay, if neither one of you is responsible, do you have any idea who *is* behind it?"

Buzz shook his head. "I can't figure it out at all. It's almost like someone is trying to make us mad at each other."

"That occurred to me too, Buzz." Mrs. Lope sighed. "Do you know of anyone who would be jealous of your friendship?"

Suddenly Buzz looked at Lorie. "You were going to nominate Melissa, remember?" he said. "She isn't mad about that, is she?"

Lorie shook her head. "No, of course not. Melissa is my best friend. Why would she want to hurt me? And she's your friend, too. She would never want to do something like that to either of us," Lorie said earnestly.

"Anyway, Melissa was only a little upset," Lorie said. "I know she wanted to be president, and she'd make a good one, but she said she thought I should have a chance, too."

"And now she's my campaign manager, and she's great," Buzz added.

"Your campaign manager?" Mrs. Lope arched her eyebrows. "That seems odd. Why didn't *you* choose her, Lorie? Didn't you say you were best friends?"

"Yes, but . . . ." Oh, boy, how was she going to explain Karen? "Karen, a new girl, spoke up before I did, and said she was manager before I had a chance, and then Melissa. . . ."

"Melissa became Buzz's assistant," Mrs. Lope finished.

No one said anything for a moment.

Finally Mrs. Lope sighed and began to stack some papers on her desk in a neat pile. "I know you must be hungry, even for cafeteria food." She smiled knowingly and Lorie began to relax a little bit. "So we're not going to pin a guilty sign on anyone today. Maybe we never will. My reason for getting you two to sit down and talk about this is to make sure nothing mean or nasty happens. Pass the message along. Fun things, yes. Mean things, no. Got that?"

Lorie nodded and so did Buzz. "Absolutely, Mrs. Lope," Lorie said. "I'll be glad when this election is over."

"I'm sorry you feel that way, Lorie," Mrs. Lope said. "It should be a wonderful experience for you. It should be a way of meeting new people, getting acquainted with the needs of your new school, and serving as one of its leaders."

"That's a big job, and I don't know if I can handle it," Lorie said.

"You never know what you can do until you try," Mrs. Lope said. Her dark eyes studied Lorie.

Buzz stood up. "Can we go now?" he asked. "I guess I am pretty hungry, even for cafeteria food."

Mrs. Lope laughed as she stood up and shook their hands. "Off you go then," she said. "And give the election all you've got. You don't have long, remember. The campaign speech assembly is next Friday."

Lorie groaned as she walked out the door. People kept reminding her that she was going to have to give a speech.

Karen and Melissa were sitting in chairs in the main office. Neither one of them looked very happy. In fact, Lorie could easily believe they'd exchanged some nasty words.

Melissa, upon seeing Lorie, jumped up and headed outside to the main corridor.

"Melissa," Lorie began, following her into the hall. "Did you have extra band practice this morning? I missed you at the corner."

"Yes, but never mind band practice." Melissa whirled on Lorie, her blue eyes cold with anger. "So . . . you think I'm responsible for everything that's been going on. Thanks a lot, Lorie." She turned and stormed off down the hall.

Lorie looked at Karen, who now stood beside her.

"I don't know where she got that idea," Karen said innocently. "Honestly, Lorie—I didn't tell her."

Nine

LORIE hurried downtown after school the following day. Her mom had asked her to go to a fabric store and pick up some material she'd ordered for the dance-recital costumes. Josh had chosen to stay next door with Mr. Higby until their mom got home. And that was okay with Lorie. She'd called Melissa and asked her to come, wanting a chance to explain yesterday's misunderstanding. After all, Lorie had never really *said* she suspected Melissa of the pranks. *But you thought it,* she reminded herself. Anyway, Melissa had curtly stated that she couldn't come and hung up. That hurt.

Now Lorie paused to look in The Best's display windows where mannequins modeled the latest coats and jackets. The jacket that Karen owned was being worn in a back-to-school scene. A feeling of envy came over Lorie as she looked at it. Karen had everything.

Suddenly she felt a tap on her shoulder. It was Karen.

"Hi, Lorie," Karen said. "Are you here to shop for clothes? I'll show you some new things that just came in."

"No, thanks. I have to go to the fabric store for my mom," Lorie replied. She knew that she really did have enough time to shop with Karen. But this morning, she felt too empty inside to do anything fun. Especially with someone other than Melissa.

"Oh," Karen replied. Then she asked the question Lorie had dreaded. "By the way, aren't you ever going to wear the barrette I gave you? I see you have another new one on today."

Lorie's face turned red. Karen noticed the brown barrette that Melissa had helped pick out at the variety store.

"Oh," Lorie said, and stopped to look at the back-to-school supplies in the stationery store window, stalling while she thought of something to say. "I'm just waiting for the right occasion to wear it." She hoped that Karen would be satisfied with that for an answer.

"What kind of an occasion?" Karen asked. "What do you mean? Can't you wear it to school?"

"Well, I just thought it needed something fancier than one of my plain skirts or jeans." Lorie felt hot. She wasn't used to telling fibs like this.

"I wish you'd wear it." Karen's wish sounded more like a command. "I bought it so you'd have a barrette that was older-looking than what you usually wear. Honestly, Lor, you look so . . . so sixth gradish."

"But I did something with my hair," Lorie began. "I pulled it back, like that girl in the magazine."

"But you only pulled it all back into a ponytail," Karen snapped back. "You need to curl it or something. Don't you have any hot rollers?"

"My mom does." Lorie felt increasingly uncomfortable. Why did Karen have to criticize constantly?

"And it seems to me you could wear some jazzier clothes," Karen went on.

"It seems to me you could stop being so bossy!" There, she'd said it out loud, and she felt better. Lorie turned and began to march toward the fabric store.

"You're pretty sensitive," Karen said, catching up. "What's the matter, can't you stand a little help?"

"I can stand a *little* but not a *lot*." Lorie

listened to the sound of her voice. It was loud, brassy, and she hated it. Maybe Karen was right. She was being overly sensitive to criticism.

They entered the fabric store and Lorie quickly purchased the material being held for her mom.

"I have to go home now," Lorie said, after she'd made her purchase.

"What's your hurry?" Karen asked. "We need to talk over some ideas for a rally. I'm going to call it the Meet Lorie Rally. We've got to do something to get your campaign going, or you're going to lose for sure."

"A rally?" Lorie's insides churned at the thought. "You mean speeches, cheers, all that?"

"Why not?" Karen began to smooth out some satiny-looking fabrics as they wandered through the store. "Just think of the attention it will get your campaign."

"That's what I'm afraid of," Lorie said under her breath. She wanted to say more—much more. She wanted to say that it was *her* campaign for president of the seventh grade class and all she wanted to do was tell the other seventh graders what kind of a president she would be if she won. Nothing else.

But with Karen, everything had to be such a

big deal. Why did Lorie always feel pressured to go along with Karen and her ideas? Why? Was it because Karen—unlike Lorie—wasn't afraid of speaking out about what she thought?

"I'll call Sandy and April and say that we're going to plan a rally and need some signs. I'll tell them what to put on the signs, okay?" Karen ran her fingers over some light blue velvet. "I'll ask Mrs. Lope for permission when I get to school in the morning. I think she'll say yes, don't you?"

Lorie shrugged. "I guess so."

"Listen." Karen hurried on. "Let's not tell Buzz and Melissa before we put the signs up for the rally. We don't want to give them ideas."

"It isn't exactly original," Lorie said.

"Maybe not, but we want to be first with it," Karen said. "Honestly, Lorie, can't you be more aggressive?"

Lorie said good-bye and hurried from the store, feeling as if she had just been scolded.

She cut through the courthouse square, then hurried across the city-college campus. Lorie didn't come this way very often. Ordinarily she walked the long way home, past the pizza parlor where kids from school hung out. Today, though, she'd settle for the shortcut and a talk with her mom.

As she waited for the traffic light to change, Lorie looked across the street to see a boy and girl walking along, laughing and talking as they held hands. It was Melissa and Bob, that eighth-grade boy who lived next door to her! What was going on? Weren't they just ordinary friends the way she and Buzz were? This didn't look ordinary though. She couldn't wait to ask Melissa. . . .

And then Lorie remembered. Melissa wasn't speaking to her.

Lorie stood on the corner as the light changed from red to green and back to red again, watching Melissa and Bob turn south on College Street. Melissa hadn't even seen her.

"Hey, Lorie, are you glued to that spot, or what?"

She glanced around to see Buzz coasting up on his bicycle. "Hi, Buzz." She didn't even smile.

"Are you on your way home?" he asked, getting off his bike. "I'll walk with you—that is, if you're still talking to me."

Good old Buzz, Lorie thought. *At least he's still my friend.* "Sure I am, silly," she said. "I was just thinking about something that I need to talk to Mom about."

He began to walk beside her. "I thought girls stopped speaking to their moms when they were about twelve, like now."

"Some girls, maybe." Lorie thought of Karen. "But not me."

"What is it?" Buzz asked. He pushed his bike around a puddle on the sidewalk.

"I really can't tell you," Lorie said.

"Girl-to-girl stuff, huh?" Buzz laughed. "It's either about boys or the election. Knowing you, it's probably the election because you don't have a boyfriend yet."

"How would you know?"

"I'd be the first to know, wouldn't I?" Buzz asked. "After all, I've known you longer than your other dippy friends, even Melissa."

"Melissa's not dippy!"

"Sorry." Buzz threw both hands into the air and his bicycle began to wobble.

"Watch it," Lorie yelled.

"Never fear." Buzz put both hands back on the handlebars again. "I guess I'll never find out what's bugging you."

Lorie wanted to laugh. "Nothing!" was all she would say.

As they reached Lorie's house, she smiled and said, "Thanks for walking with me, Buzz." She backed toward her house as she spoke, hoping her mom was already home and could talk.

"Any time," Buzz said. "And hey . . . don't

look so serious, okay?"

Lorie tried to sound cheerful and smile, but had trouble pulling it off. "I'm worried about my terrible responsibility," she called to him. "If I don't beat you in the election, our class will have a nerd for a president, you know?"

"Oh, yeah?" Buzz yelled. He started to put his bike down on the grass.

"I have to go inside now." Lorie laughed quickly. "My talk with Mom, remember?"

"Excuses, excuses," he yelled as he rode down the street.

Lorie hurried around the house and inside the back door.

"Hi, Lorie." Mrs. Scott was in the kitchen. "I was beginning to worry. What kept you?" She took the package from Lorie and opened it.

"Oh, I ran into people, things like that." Lorie threw her jacket on a chair. "Mom, can we talk now?"

"Sure, honey. What's the matter?" Her mom glanced up before she began to unfold the bright green fabric.

Lorie took a deep breath and plunged ahead about her problems, especially with Karen.

Her mom listened quietly until Lorie finished. "Well, you have to decide if the barrette is a gift you feel comfortable accepting. If not, you should return it, don't you think? And maybe you should pay for all the paints and paper and markers that Karen has bought. Do you think an advance on your allowance will do it?"

Lorie sighed. "That's what I thought, too. I left the barrette in my locker at school, but I think I'd like to pay for the supplies right now and get it over with."

"Good idea." Mrs. Scott located her purse behind a sack of groceries on the counter and handed her some bills. "Is this enough?"

"A little more, Mom. Karen bought a lot."

Her mom said nothing, but handed over more money. *That's the great thing about her,* Lorie thought—*she's understanding.*

"I'm going to ride over to Karen's house," Lorie said. "I should be back in 20 minutes or so." Lorie started out the back door, then stopped. "And thanks, Mom. Thanks a lot."

Ten

KAREN'S house looked like a castle to Lorie when she first saw it in the distance. Then, as she rode closer, it looked like something that might be shown on television in one of those nighttime soap operas her mom watched sometimes. The nearer she got, the larger the house became.

Lorie rode up the circular driveway and leaned her bike against a bush before walking up some white stone steps to the front door. The door was huge. Lorie looked up to see a fan-shaped window glistening above it.

She rang the doorbell and listened as a series of bells played inside. Suddenly a voice spoke to her. It was Mrs. Bradley, but she was nowhere to be seen.

"Well, hello, Lorie," Mrs. Bradley said. "May I help you?"

"Hello," Lorie said, looking around. Where

was that voice coming from anyway? "I came to see Karen. Only for just a minute though."

The door opened. "Come in, dear," Mrs. Bradley said in person. "If you'll wait here in the hall, I'll find Karen for you."

Lorie stepped inside and watched as Mrs. Bradley walked out of sight at the end of a long hall. Then she began to look around. Even though Mrs. Bradley called this room a hall, it looked the size of a living room to Lorie. Black and white tiles covered the floor. *Wouldn't Josh have fun playing giant checkers on them?* she thought. A glittery chandelier with lots of mirrored pieces hung over a black, marble-topped table. Lorie stared and stared, wondering if anyone could see her now, the way Mrs. Bradley had seen her right through the front door.

Mrs. Bradley returned, her shoes making click-clack sounds on the tile. More click-clacks followed and then Karen appeared.

"Hi, Lorie," she said. "Let's go back to my room."

Lorie breathed a deep sigh. "This house is so huge," she whispered as they walked down another hall, quieted with thick carpet. "It must be fun to live here. I'll bet you can play your tapes as loud as you want to and your folks won't even hear it."

"You want to bet?" Karen snapped. "I can't do anything I want to."

Karen opened a door and Lorie caught her breath as she stared. The walls, chairs, bedspreads, and drapes of Karen's bedroom were covered in a green and pink flowery fabric. The carpet was plain green, and it felt as if it were three inches thick.

"It's beautiful," Lorie whispered. "It looks like a magazine picture!"

"That's what it's supposed to look like," Karen said. "Mom saw this picture and decided that's what my room would look like. Did you want to work on the election plans?"

"I can't stay very long," Lorie said, sinking into the fluffy bedspread. "I just came to pay you for all the supplies you bought."

"Forget it." Karen walked over to a white desk and took some papers from a drawer. "Look, I've been working on some ideas for the Meet Lorie Rally. We need to make signs."

Lorie unbuttoned her jacket a little and took her wallet from an inside pocket. "Not until we settle what I owe you, Karen. I want to pay for all of it." Lorie suddenly felt as if a huge weight had been lifted from her shoulders.

Karen bounced on the bed. "Well, okay, but I don't know what the fuss is all about."

Suddenly Mrs. Bradley walked in. "Karen,"

she said. "How many times have I told you not to sit on the bed like that? You'll crush the spread!"

"Yes, Mother," Karen said, standing up.

Mrs. Bradley smiled at Lorie as she smoothed out the spread. "Do you like Karen's room?"

"It's pretty," Lorie began. "Um . . . I have to go home," she added quickly, before she blurted out what she really thought. Yes, it was pretty—but not comfortable. Definitely not a place where a girl could bring her friends and have fun.

"Don't go," Karen said. "We haven't worked on the rally yet."

"Mom will worry if I'm not back soon." Lorie started down the long hall.

Karen followed her outside and watched while Lorie turned her bicycle around to face the driveway. "Lorie?" she whispered. "Please don't tell anyone about my mom."

Lorie looked up to see Karen standing in the doorway. She looked so little standing there, and kind of lonesome, too.

* * * * *

April and Sandy were waiting beside Lorie's locker the next morning. "We don't mean to complain, Lorie," April began. "But Karen called us last night and said we had to have all these signs put up by noon today."

"And all of these balloons blown up by tomorrow so we can give them away at the Meet Lorie Rally," Sandy finished.

Lorie turned from her locker to look at them. April's dark ponytail had come loose from its bow, and Sandy had smudge marks on her nose.

"We've been here an hour," Sandy went on. "But Karen didn't show up."

"When did she bring the signs over to you?" Lorie asked, wondering when Karen had time to do them.

"She didn't print them. We did," April said. "But she told us what to say."

"It seems to me you might have helped a little," Sandy said. "After all, it's your election."

Lorie opened her mouth, then closed it quickly, hoping that what she said next wouldn't sound like a lame excuse. "I didn't know Karen's plans would move this quickly. I didn't even know for sure that we were going to have a rally. We've only talked about it so far."

But she knew those really were only excuses. *I should have been doing all the planning myself,* Lorie thought. *I should have been leading, not following. What kind of a president am I going to make?*

"Anyway, you're both right," she said, taking the signs from them. "Let's put this stuff in my locker. I'll tell Karen we'll *all* work on them after school."

April sighed. "Thanks, Lorie. That's only fair."

As soon as they left, Lorie quickly read the signs. The rally was scheduled for tomorrow, right after school, on the library steps. The timing was good, the place was perfect, but the star of the show was all wrong.

Melissa should have been the candidate, not me, Lorie thought. *How did I ever get into this?*

But then she remembered—she'd been too timid to say no.

Karen didn't appear at all that morning. At first Lorie worried that nothing would be done for the rally tomorrow, but then she realized that she could do the work with Sandy and April's help. In fact, Karen's presence wasn't needed at all. Strangely, though, Lorie did miss her a little.

At noon, Lorie filled her tray in the cafeteria line, then looked around for an empty place at a table. This was the first time she had come here without someone to sit with. She suddenly felt overcome with shyness. How could she sit down at a table with kids she didn't know and talk to them? *Why did Karen have to get sick today?* Lorie thought.

Lorie spotted Melissa seated next to Bob way over on the other side of the room. Then she remembered that they weren't speaking, and besides, it didn't matter now anyway. Melissa probably wasn't interested in being best friends with her anymore, especially now that she had a boyfriend.

"Lorie. Lorie."

She saw April and Sandy waving at her from a table in the middle of the room and breathed a deep sigh. She hurried over and sat down.

"Am I glad to see you," she said. "I thought I wasn't going to see anyone I know."

"Aren't you friends with Melissa anymore?" Sandy asked, taking a big bite of her hot dog.

"Oh, sure," Lorie tried to sound confident. "It's just that . . . that. . . ."

"She's got a boyfriend, you mean," April said, pointing over her shoulder toward the table where Melissa sat with Bob.

"An eighth grader too," Sandy said after a glance. "Wow!"

Lorie bit into her hot dog without tasting it. Why hadn't Melissa told her what was going on? she wondered. She could have hinted at least. Being best friends seemed so easy last year. Now, suddenly, everything seemed to change—especially the friend she thought she knew so well.

Buzz pulled out a chair and sat down across from her, his tray loaded with extras of everything, even brownies. "Hi, women," he said, his voice cracking in the middle of the words.

Sandy and April began to laugh as Buzz's face turned bright pink. *Even Buzz's voice is changing,* Lorie thought.

"Where's Karen?" he asked when Sandy and April were finally quiet. "Don't tell me you've escaped her clutches."

"I guess she's sick," Lorie said. "She hasn't been in school today."

"What are you going to do after school then?" Buzz asked, digging into his macaroni and cheese.

"Sandy and April and I are going to put up signs for my rally tomorrow afternoon."

Buzz looked up, interested. "A rally? That's a good idea. Was it yours?"

"No, Karen's. She's good at thinking up things to do." And Lorie realized she meant it. Karen really did have good ideas. If only she wasn't so bossy . . . .

"After you put up the signs, then what are you going to do?" Buzz persisted.

Sandy and April were listening intently. "I guess I'm just going home, Buzz. Why?"

"Well . . ." Buzz paused. "I thought we ought to work on the speeches we have to give in assembly, so maybe we should . . . ." All at once he noticed April and Sandy staring at him. "Never mind," he said, standing up and picking up his tray. "I'll see you later."

"But you didn't finish eating," Lorie called after him. "I wonder if he's getting sick, too," she said, watching him put his still-filled tray on the cart and walk out. "Maybe there's something going around."

"There's something going around all right," Sandy said, sounding mysterious and glancing over at Melissa and Bob again.

Lorie looked at her, puzzled. "What are you talking about?"

Sandy and April just looked at each other and smiled.

Oh, no, Lorie thought. *They don't think he has a crush on me, do they?*

Eleven

WHEN Lorie walked in the house after school, she heard the telephone ringing in the hall above the din of the television in the family room.

"Why don't you ever answer the phone, Josh?" she yelled as she raced for it. "Oh, never mind. Hello?"

"Hi, Lorie," her mom said. "I'm running a few minutes late and wanted to make sure you were home with Josh. Are you hungry?"

Lorie mumbled, "No, I can wait till you get home." She had too much on her mind right now to think about food.

"Is everything all right, Lor?" Mom asked.

"Oh, sure, fine."

"Okay. I'll see you in a little while."

Lorie hung up, realizing that she didn't even want to discuss this new problem with her mom. *How weird,* she thought. *I've always told*

Mom about everything that happens.

How should she act around Buzz now? If he liked her—like April and Sandy thought—then what was she supposed to do?

Melissa was the one whose advice she needed. Melissa knew her better than anyone, and now she even had a little experience in the boy department. But she wasn't at all sure if Melissa would talk to her.

What about Karen? She could talk to boys easily. Maybe she could give Lorie some advice, too. Lorie decided to call her.

She dialed Karen's number and waited. Would she be too sick to come to the telephone?

"Hello," a quavery voice said.

"Karen, is that you?" Lorie could hardly recognize her voice.

"Lorie." Karen sounded a little weak. "I've been hoping you'd call."

"I was just wondering how you were feeling."

"Better, now. I had an upset stomach in the middle of the night. I hope you don't get it just before the rally and everything. Did you get the signs put up?"

"Yes. Sandy and April and I put them up all over school. Kids have been asking questions, so we think a lot of them will come."

"That's neat," Karen said.

"But I'm scared." There, it was out in the open at last.

"My dad says he's always nervous before he has to give a speech too," Karen said.

"Really?"

"He says a speech won't be any good if the speaker isn't a little nervous."

"Then my speech will be the best one ever given," Lorie said. She began to feel a little better about the rally and the speech assembly as well.

"Lorie?" Karen hesitated. "Lorie, about yesterday, when you came to my house . . . now you know why I didn't invite you over before."

"But, Karen, your house is really gorgeous." Lorie hoped she sounded convincing.

"Oh, sure. But it's not a very fun place, is it? Not like your house." Karen's voice grew stronger, and a little angry. "I can't even fix my room how I want it. My mother always has to have things her way. It's always 'Do this. Don't do that!' I really hate it!"

"I know what you mean, Karen," Lorie replied. "*Nobody* likes to be told by someone what to do all the time."

Karen didn't say anything for a moment. Then she sighed. "You're talking about me, aren't you? I guess I can get to be a little pushy. I'm sorry. I just really want you to win the campaign."

"It's okay," Lorie said. "Look, do you think you'll be back at school tomorrow?"

"I'm not sure. Mom says I have to start eating before I can go to school."

"I sure hope you eat something then because I want your help at the rally."

"You do?" Karen asked, sounding surprised. "You really want me there?"

"Yes," Lorie answered. "I really do."

"I'm going to eat something right now."

After Lorie said good-bye, she realized that she hadn't talked about Buzz—but it didn't matter. She sure felt a lot better about Karen.

Lorie hurried into the family room where the television was blasting away. "Josh, don't you have homework or something else to do? Those cartoons will stunt your growth."

"You sound just like Mom," he said, yawning. "There's nothing else to do."

Someone began to knock at the back door. "I'll bet that's Mr. Higby," Josh said as he ran to the door. "I'll get it."

"Good," Lorie answered. She walked down the hall and into her room, then quickly changed into her faded jeans and stretched-out sweatshirt.

Josh poked his head in the door of her

room. "It wasn't Mr. Higby," he said, chewing on a celery stalk.

"Well . . . who was it?" Lorie grunted as she stooped to pick up some clothes.

"Just somebody. He's down there waiting to see you." Josh said as he disappeared into his own room.

What? Lorie thought, racing to the kitchen. *Who could . . . .*

There was Buzz, standing by the sink with his Dodgers cap twisted up in his hands.

"Hi, Lorie," he began. Lorie noticed that his hair was combed. That was a first. "I just thought . . . I just thought I'd come over."

Lorie found herself wondering what to say. Everything seemed stiff—she suddenly felt self-conscious, too. Why did she have to be wearing these ugly jeans and shirt?

"Do you want something to eat?" she asked. Buzz could always manage to stuff down some calories.

"I'm not hungry." Buzz shifted back and forth uneasily. "If you're busy, I can come back some other time."

Lorie shook her head and said "No, I'm not busy. Why don't we sit down at the table?" *This sure is different,* she thought. *This is the first time I've ever invited Buzz to sit down as if he were a real guest.*

"I was thinking," Buzz began. His voice cracked and he cleared his throat. "We ought to work on the speeches we're going to give in assembly so we won't say the same thing."

"Okay." Lorie pushed the salt and pepper shakers over by the sugar bowl. "You go first. What are you going to say?"

"Well, I think we ought to have new drinking fountains out by the gym," Buzz said. "In fact, I think the drinking fountains ought to be inside the locker rooms instead of in the hall."

"One for the boys and one for the girls," Lorie said. "That's a good idea."

"That way, when you come in from P.E., you can get a drink even while you're all sweaty and dirty and don't have to worry what you look like."

Another first, Lorie thought. *Buzz is worrying about being seen sweaty and dirty.* "How much do you think this will cost?" she asked, remembering her dad's question.

"I don't know. But I guess I'd better find out, huh? Hey, what's the rally thing all about?"

"It was really Karen's idea."

"Do you like it?"

"Yes," Lorie admitted. "But I'm not much good at making speeches and leading cheers. The rally might not be very good."

"You can do it, Lorie. I'm going to come to it," Buzz told her seriously.

"But you're the opposition, Buzz. You shouldn't come to my rally."

"But I want to."

Suddenly Lorie was suspicious. Buzz was being so nice. "You're not planning anything, are you?"

"What do you mean?" He looked so innocent.

"Like doing something crazy when I'm talking?"

"Lorie, I don't do stupid stuff like that anymore." Buzz looked so sincere when he spoke. "Being in seventh grade is serious. It's a whole new way of life."

Lorie studied him for a moment. "Well, okay." But she still wasn't sure. He was right about one thing though. Seventh grade *was* a whole new way of life.

* * * * *

Lorie found a note sticking out of her locker the next morning. "All candidates report to the nurse's office for an emergency meeting right after school," it said. It was signed with some initials she couldn't make out. The principal's?

Lorie turned the note over in her hands. This sure was a weird note. And what about her rally? She'd have to give some instructions to Sandy and April about handing out balloons, leading a couple of cheers they'd made up, and keeping things moving until she could get there.

Lorie hurried to homeroom and saw Karen already in her seat. "Am I ever glad to see you," Lorie said. "Look at this note. You'll have to take charge of the rally until I arrive."

Karen read the note and looked puzzled. "Who's it from?"

Lorie shrugged. "Must be Mrs. Lope. She's the only one who would call all the candidates together."

"But why in the nurse's office?"

Lorie thought a moment, then replied. "I don't know. Maybe it's a very special meeting that she doesn't want anyone to know about."

"That makes sense, I guess," Karen said. "I think you're probably right. But what is it about? Did something happen yesterday when I was absent? Were more posters defaced?"

"No, but maybe she's found out who defaced mine and Buzz's. Maybe she's going to have the person confess."

"I'll come with you," Karen said.

"No, you'd better stay at the rally," Lorie

said. "You'll be needed there."

At noon Lorie ate lunch with Sandy and April and Karen, discussing the rally. Once, as Lorie stopped talking long enough to have a sip of milk, she looked up and saw Melissa watching. Lorie smiled. She couldn't help it, smiling at Melissa was the most natural thing in the world.

And then Melissa smiled back. She actually smiled and then she waved. Bob, seated next to Melissa, grinned. *Oh, great! Melissa must not be angry anymore,* Lorie thought.

* * * * *

After school, Lorie raced to her locker, combed her hair, and hurried down to the nurse's office. No one else was around yet, so she leaned against the wall and watched kids as they walked past. Buzz should be coming along any minute, as well as the other candidates.

A few minutes passed. She wondered if the others could be inside the nurse's office already. But when she tried the door it was locked. Now what? No one else was coming this way. Could she have misread the note? She searched around in her purse and found the crumpled piece of paper. No, it said the nurse's office after school today.

Lorie decided to go to the principal's office. Maybe the meeting had been changed and they'd forgotten to mention it to her. She brushed through a crowd of eighth graders coming her way. One of them said, "Where's your mustache, Lorie?" but she pretended that she didn't hear. At least that person knew her name, if only from a ruined poster.

She opened the door to the principal's office and went inside. A secretary looked up from her typing and said, "Yes, can I help you?"

"I'm not sure," Lorie began. "I got this note today." Then she explained what had happened.

"No one from this office sent that note," the secretary said. "I think someone may have played a trick on you."

"But why?" Lorie wondered out loud. Then she understood. Someone had lured her away from the rally. She should have been there right now, this minute. Instead she was trying to find a meeting that didn't exist.

Lorie ran from the office, down the long hall to the library and out the door to the steps. Sandy and April were running after some students and trying to give them balloons while Karen watched.

"We couldn't keep them here any longer,"

Karen said when she saw Lorie. "They said they came to hear you, and when you didn't show up, they just left. Where have you been?"

"On a wild goose chase," Lorie said. She explained it all to Karen and then to Sandy and April as they came to stand beside her. "And I know who did it, too," Lorie finished.

Twelve

LORIE was still angry the next morning as she walked out the door and headed for school. *Wait until I see Buzz,* she thought. *He played up to me just so he could ruin my rally. Some friend.*

As she neared the corner of Lorain and Wembly, Lorie slowed her steps out of habit. Since third grade she had met Melissa right here at this spot and they had walked to school together. *Not anymore,* she thought glumly. She really missed her friend.

She paused at the curb, looked down Wembly and couldn't believe it. There was Melissa, running toward her and waving frantically.

"Wait," Melissa called. Her long, blond hair was blown into tangles as she finally caught up with Lorie. "I've been wanting to talk to you alone, Lor." She paused to catch her breath.

"It's so important," Melissa said breathlessly.

"You're not mad anymore?" Lorie asked.

"Mad?" Melissa looked puzzled. "I thought *you* were mad."

"Not me." Lorie shook her head. "After that day in the principal's office when you said . . . ."

"I've been wanting to explain about that." Melissa pulled in a deep breath. "Karen didn't come right out and say you accused me of defacing the posters," Melissa said. "I think I jumped to a big conclusion because I was jealous."

"Of Karen?" Lorie asked. "No way. I think we're going to be good friends, but you're still my best friend . . . that is, if you still want to be best friends."

"Oh, yes, I want to be best friends." Melissa shook her tangled hair away from her face. "I was afraid you wouldn't want to be, though, after the way I acted."

"And I thought you might not want to be anymore because of your boyfriend. I guess he's your boyfriend." Lorie didn't know if that was a question or a statement.

Melissa's face turned pink. "Oh, you mean Bob? Lorie, it's so exciting to have a boy like me—especially an older guy."

"Tell me about it," Lorie said as they began

to walk to school together.

"I will, but then you'd better tell me about Buzz, too. I've noticed the way he looks at you."

"Oh, that." Lorie's tone matched the anger she felt now. "I'm so mad at him."

"About what?"

Quickly Lorie told her about the note. "So you see, all that buttering up to me was phoney baloney."

"No! Wait until I tell you something that Bob told me," Melissa said.

"About Buzz?"

"No, about the pranks that have been played on you *and* Buzz."

Melissa paused and Lorie thought she'd explode from waiting.

"Bob said some eighth graders decided to have a little fun because they know how serious seventh graders are about their first elections at junior high. So a couple of those guys drew pictures on your posters and changed the words."

"Really? They're the ones who did that?"

Melissa nodded. "Then they did the same thing to Buzz's posters and sat back to see what would happen."

"That's awful." Lorie gave a pile of leaves a kick. "Who are they?"

"Bob wouldn't say. I guess he didn't want to rat on them so that it would get back to Mrs. Lope."

"What about the note? Did they do that, too?"

"Yes. Bob told me last night when he came over. I wanted to call you after he left, but Mom said it was too late. I'm so glad I caught you this morning before you got to school."

"Me, too," Lorie said. "I was about to tell Buzz off."

"I know," Melissa said.

"Oh, Melissa, I'm so mixed up about this boy stuff. How do you know when they mean what they say or what they don't say?"

"It's hard. I guess you just try to figure it out as you go along."

"I'm trying to figure out a lot of things," Lorie said. "But I'm getting better. Especially at making friends with different people."

"But being best friends with just one person is best," Melissa added.

Lorie smiled at Melissa, feeling better about junior high than she had since she'd started. Now all she had to worry about was the speech assembly tomorrow.

* * * * *

Karen came home from school with Lorie, and they worked on the speech together. By the time Mrs. Bradley came for Karen at 5:00, Lorie was sure her speech would be the best. Also, Lorie was impressed. She could tell that Karen had been careful not to be bossy.

"Don't worry about a thing," Karen said, gathering up her books and papers.

"Before you go," Lorie said. "There's something I want to give you." She ran to her room and took the box containing the hair barrette out of its hiding place. She'd brought it home a couple of days ago, waiting for just the right moment to return it to Karen. Now seemed to be the time.

Lorie hurried back into the kitchen and gave the box to Karen. "Thanks, Karen, but I really can't accept this. It's beautiful but . . . it isn't me."

Karen looked at Lorie, then at her mother who was waiting just inside the door of the kitchen. "I'm sorry, Lorie, I just . . . well, I guess you're right. I didn't have to give you the barrette."

"Oh, but it's nice to give gifts to friends," Mrs. Bradley threw in. "And you have certainly been a special friend to Karen, Lorie."

Lorie smiled. "Karen's been a good friend to me, too." She felt a lot better now. "Anyway,"

Lorie continued, "Maybe I'll be ready to wear something that fancy when I'm older. Save it for my sixteenth birthday, okay, Karen?"

Karen smiled back at Lorie. "Okay—it's a deal!"

As Lorie closed the door behind Karen and Mrs. Bradley, she remembered the poster in Mr. Crawford's room. Be yourself. *I'm trying,* she thought happily, *I'm trying.*

* * * * *

The next morning right after roll was taken in homeroom, the seventh-grade class filed into the auditorium. Lorie was glad that she didn't have to wait any longer.

The candidates walked out onstage together a few minutes after the rest of the class was seated. Lorie sat next to Buzz and smiled at him. He smiled back, but from a million miles away. She could tell his mind was on his speech. She decided that her mind should be on her speech, too.

But there was so much else to think about— like all those students in the audience. She could see their faces, rows and rows of them, all looking this way. *I don't know if I can do this,* she thought, her stomach beginning to churn. *But I have to.* Then she remembered something both her dad and Mrs. Lope had said. *You'll never know what you can do until you try.*

Mrs. Lope stood up and gave an introductory speech about responsibility, fair play, and good sportsmanship. *Why doesn't she hurry?* Lorie thought.

Then a boy who was running for student council stood up and began to talk. Lorie tried to listen but she kept looking at her own notes, wondering if she should try to change something here, say it more clearly there.

Before she knew it, it was time for Buzz to talk. He stood up, walked to the podium, and without any notes at all, began to speak about his goals for the coming year. When he came to the part about the drinking fountains in the locker rooms of the gym, applause broke out all over the auditorium.

Everyone must feel the same way, Lorie thought. He even had the cost of the fountains memorized and rattled off numbers as if he had a computer in his head. When he sat down a few minutes later, he received the loudest and longest applause of any candidate yet.

Then Mrs. Lope called Lorie's name. It was time.

She stood up and walked slowly to the

microphone, wondering if she dared not look at her notes while speaking. She knew everything she was going to say, so why use notes? Do what Buzz had done.

Lorie started to put her note cards down on the podium, but somehow she missed. The cards sailed all over the floor, drifting out of reach. Giggles erupted all over the auditorium. She waited long, agonizing seconds until everyone finally settled down.

"Now you know my secret," she said. "I'm so nervous, I'm klutzy. This is my first speech and from the way it's going, it may be my last."

Everyone began to laugh. *I'm not the only one who has felt this way,* she thought, smiling. Then she went on to tell about replacing the bicycle rack and how much it would cost and voting for ice-cream flavor of the week in the cafeteria. That brought a few cheers.

"In conclusion," she said, "I'd just like to say that I'd make the best president possible. I'd like to say that, but I'm not sure. If you elect me, we'll all just have to wait and see what I can do. I can't make many promises, but I can make one. If elected, I'll do my best."

Buzz was still clapping as she sat down. Lorie felt pleased about what she'd said. It wasn't exactly what she'd planned, but it would do.

* * * * *

Elections were held that afternoon. Buzz's victory was announced the next morning during homeroom. "It was close," Mr. Crawford announced. "Very close."

"Congratulations, Buzz," Lorie said, when she saw him at noon in the cafeteria. "I think you're going to make a terrific president."

"Thanks, Lor." His grin split his face in half. "You would have been great, too. And you really helped me with my speech. If it hadn't been for you, I never would have thought of getting the costs of the drinking fountain from the school's vice-principal."

Other seventh graders came up to Buzz now and surrounded him with their congratulations. Lorie took her tray and sat down next to Karen. A moment later, Melissa sat down across from them.

"Where's . . . you know?" Lorie asked.

"Bob and I don't have to be together every second," Melissa said, taking a bite of her sandwich. "Even if we are going steady."

"Going steady?" Karen asked. "That's neat, Melissa."

"Wow," added Lorie. "Well, Melissa, we have lots of stuff to talk about."

"Any time." Melissa smiled at both of them. "I always have time for my friends."

"Speaking of friends," Buzz said, placing his tray down across from Lorie, "would my loyal subjects mind if I joined them?"

The three girls groaned and then Lorie spoke up. "Sure, as long as you remember you're only president and not king."

"By the way, Melissa," Buzz looked at her. "Thanks for your help."

"Sure, any year." Melissa grinned. "Only next year, let's remember not to make fun of the 'serious' seventh graders!"

Lorie, Buzz, and Karen laughed along with Melissa.

"*And*," said Lorie, "next year Melissa and I are on the same side."

"Does that mean you'll be running for eighth-grade class president?" Karen asked.

"Well," Lorie answered, "there's only one way to find out. Wait until next year!" And to herself Lorie thought, *But first I'm going to enjoy this one!*

About the Author

ELIZABETH VAN STEENWYK has written over forty books for young people and more than one hundred articles and short stories for adults' and children's magazines. She has also written and produced many radio and television programs for children.

Elizabeth was born in Galesburg, Illinois. Galesburg is the hometown of Carl Sandburg. Elizabeth read many of Sandburg's books at an early age.

"Students growing up there inherited a literary legacy," she has said. "That early influence gave me the hope that I, too, could become a writer one day. Fortunately, that's all I've ever done and I couldn't have wished for more."

When she is not writing, Elizabeth enjoys traveling with her husband to far-off places. She also enjoys backpacking California's High Sierra, reading history and biography, and tap dancing.

Elizabeth and her husband have lived in San Marino, California, for many years. They are the parents of four grown children.